tight
little
vocal
cords

a novel
loie rawding

KERNPUNKT • PRESS

Book Design: Jesi Buell
Art and Cover Design: Laurie Smithwick

1st Printing: 2020

ISBN-13 978-1-7323251-8-0

KERNPUNKT Press Hamilton,

New York 13346

www.kernpunktpress.com

For Mom

Some will say he's gone mad; others will look and say he's looked in at the lattices of Heaven and come back with the madness of splendor on him.

Marsden Hartley

BOOK I.

WERE WE WERE THERE

ORIGIN

M will be born many times over, always in a solitary space where shadows roll with the sound of waves and the winter is long with night. He submits himself to each landscape, to the rush and bind of branches, water, and gale force. A kiss, for example. His lips, the same grain as the trees. These kinds of carved wooden tools, shaped by iron, held with nails that dimple skin into corroded silver. A kiss. What happens if he gets left in the rain?

Nothing new may come of this. A life flips in space. Another is pressed by the wave. To reveal any truth, will mean to repeat the lines that are drawn around him. Each time, pressing fingerprints into his blue eyes, causing a ripple in his witness.

M was born from his mother's house, her body stretched with and within a frame built by his father. Her walls of skin, tight and dry, stand hard in rooms of wainscoting. A puzzle bound together with old things. He emerged with a grotesque sound. *Silence.* A work of abstraction. A smudge against his mother's breast. How easy it is to forget: grapevines can grow through cliffs.

Was he wanted? They stoically place him in a wooden cradle that trips on a crack in the floor, as it tries to rock back and forth without the push of a bare foot. The child, M, hums along with the hitch of it. His heart beats again and again, but does anyone notice the *thud?*

The clouds become mirrors, then music. He stacks flat rocks to the beat of gull's wings, forming a seawall around his sunny wasteland.

M is born in a ring formed from shale and filled with sand. Dried beach peas line his bedside. In the morning, a humid mist rises from the water still smelling of the night's cold.

He rises from restless sleep and walks to low tide, feeds off salty cattail roots, crab apples, sour grapes as green as the vine. Men and women surround him, trying so hard to remain only as far as they've gotten. A community existing on just enough, pushed to the edge of cliffs on which they balance with locked knees, floating away from a flickering world.

His long silences leave empty parenthesis around his mother.

The only thing he knows of his father are two long arms that chop wood and drop the stacks of dead limbs into an old milk crate by the stove. The father always smells of burning, his hair the color of ash and peeling birch bark is his skin.

The mother always takes a standing position to piss, same as how she stands over her child. Her biggest fear was that she would have a girl child, more beautiful, more powerful than herself. A child more able to leave, to go beyond the cage, and take all she may ever want.

She was given M, who might yet prove to be exactly this. She periodically chops off her hair, with her eyes closed, asking her son to what degree she might be judged a work of art. She sings to him at night about setting her curves on fire with tongues of the deepest currents. His mother is sculpted from hard granite. His father is the white water that thrashes at her ankles and polishes the surface of her stomach.

M and his mother wrap around each other, forcing their bodies through his father's rough wake. The father needs them to stay, to join this local circle of bait and catch, salt swept pine needles and a horizon the same color as the ocean pressing against it.

No matter where he goes, M will see the sun through many grains of sand. Such glitter dots and slashes across his vision, forming a line of broken images. He will swallow these demons one by one, but in this beginning, the shine of it all makes him smile his first kind of smile.

He leans forward, the child his mother feared, always hungry, breathing through the wet O his mouth makes at rest. A rosebud that never blooms. A hole, like the one left in the bloody earth after his birth.

He will venture out on the road she never saw, searching for the scattered pieces of a self, always using the twisted laws, the tortured tools, of his mother. M forgot that his father existed until she disappeared.

LINEA NIGRA

M admires and desires the woman in his mother's form. Such is the impact of her velvety touch. Yet, she remains untouchable, protected by her thinning dark hair and pale armor composed of a deceptively thick skin. So, he sticks his child hands tightly between his knees and then behind his ears, seeking out his own smell, which came from her.

No translation is required.

Need or want or always, what is the taste of words like these? Translation is always required.

M still craves his mother in part because he didn't get to see her die. When he was finally allowed to enter the room all that remained was a few empty skirts standing in the middle of the room, and a deeper silence. And a blue tin cup speckled with white, by her pillow, half full of the pulpy seaweed she drank as tea, now cold. The sourness of it stung his lips.

As many mothers do, she left deep scratches in his skin. See M: still young, walking with the limp of new legs, knees the size of elbows that shake in the wind. His mother is laughing at the ocean, pressing her body into the horizon of ships headed for other countries. She is talking to an invisible sailor who has joined them for their daily walk. The man seems to be asking with some quality of knowledge, *just give me a taste of that skin. Just there, please oh, those sweet, perky tits.* His voice is the sound of a storm moving off shore, coaxing her into the surf, demanding her devotion for just a little while. She seems inclined to give in, the clouds tugging at her hand while the other remains locked onto his.

M is used to this flirtation and much more interested in the sand breathing beneath him. Oval shaped cells bubble up, surging between his toes, clear drool emerging from holes that pop from the porous tissue. He calls out, *please oh, look. Look between my sweet, perky toes.* His mother reacts instantly, as if she heard his voice before he opened his mouth. With a single gesture she digs her thumb and fore finger into one of the opened pores. M is knocked down beside the widening gap. The sand growing wetter with each flex of the muscle in her forearm. He breathes through his teeth, through the O that his lips make. One of his eyelashes is caught inside out. After humming and digging for several minutes, his mother grasps something solid. She grips it like the head of a bullet that must come out and tugs at the ground, her other hand flat in a pool of sandy water, keeping her steady.

A head the size of a thumbnail appears from the wound, then a thousand legs on a black soaked body. The massive worm is very much alive and reacts instantly, coiling itself around her fingers, gripping her wrist like a damp leather strap. He sees the pleasure of tightening muscle under its thin skin. M stops breathing.

She disentangles the thing from herself and lets it fall onto his body. The thousand legs animate in tiny, moving circles, each wheelhouse working to crawl up his leg. This is a significant moment. He wonders if it is possible to be pulled back into the creature's hole, sealed into the lung of the beach, his whole body wrapped in its rust lined scales. To forever join this precious, powerful thing. This thing of cold-blooded muscle, with only an open mouth and no eyes.

Dear M,

I am asking myself why? Why this? Why now? Who fucking cares? And while no answer comes to mind, I can only say that I am using you to understand myself. I am trying to make sense of our memories. You remind me of my own hesitant brashness. Embarrassed, I enact this composition anyway. I want to translate what is written behind the iron-backed mirror at the end of the hall and the impacts we can cause together.

I am writing my way into wandering, like you. Who is making the decisions? Who transcribes these rules and why should I listen? Why do you keep reading? There are so many stories I still don't know. The lives of our makers are so unclear. I'm wandering, just like you, pretending to know. I am just beginning and I am using you.

I keep waking up with my hands in fists. I am pulled into the dirt of our histories for what? To grasp whatever meaning I can salvage. Could be nothing at all. Could mean everything.

Meanwhile, there's this young bitch laughing at me from up a tree just outside my window. You know the one, the wide pine that leans toward the east. She won't come down or talk to me the way I need her to, which is why I can't help but talk to you. She's just another piece of us that I can't shake loose, that I can't shake free.

Yours truly,

TERRA DISFORMA

The remoteness of M's home gives it a false sense of perpetuity. Again, and again, and again, the fishermen slide up to the dock, slick with the wet feet of swimmers and mackerel intestines splattered across rotting board. Abandoned fish hooks stick up from the cracks. Lines of waves crest over cliffs shaped like broad men's thighs, hairy with Atlantic sea moss, strong and resolute against the wind.

The line of the island forms a crotch. Before her departure, his mother holds her own with both hands and says, *this is power. This is where we live.* But his father just calls it stone, and returns to toeing a line between their small portion of rocky beach and the dingy he uses to fish. Shards of glass collect on this beach, thrown back from the tide, pieces broken to fit between a child's toes. There is more of that rare blue kind here than anywhere else on the island, it is rocked to a fine smoothness, dusted with salt, bleached by the sun.

The island is an idle rock with a breeze that keeps the black flies away. No need for shoes, except required to get into the amusement park built by a retired tycoon. The park seduces its crowds with stale fried dough, painted rocks, chipped buoy mobiles. All of it gift wrapped in relentless and nauseating splashes of fun. A rainbow of smashed light bulbs.

On one side of the mirror, M's place of birth is a sunken ship, split in two, all of her degenerate crew lost and long forgotten. On the other side, it is a funhouse freshly painted every June with the sweat of the rich, buttery lobster shells, and sour gin.

It starts here because it ends here.

STILL LIFE

On the day his mother dies:

> The house blows itself open with a gust of wind and still his father won't let him see behind the door. The whole house cracks in the wind and salt, paint chipping across the sill and window frames sinking into the plaster wall. Everything is splitting. The sun is silver bright behind a fog curtain. Black sand, shining with oil from Fisherman's Cove, blows itself inside, forming sacrificial mounds at the foot of every bed and bookshelf. Except hers, her door is closed and his father will not let him in.

Grains of sand snag the rugs and scratch the tops of his feet. They grind between his molars. Dry sea grass inflames his bare legs. It whips through, pulled from the ground by relentless gusts. He is left with a collage of paper cuts across his skin. He can see his veins throbbing underneath. He has to leave, to go somewhere not here. Giving up, he walks through the dry, low tide as the storm finally moves out. The damp air is slowing down. It makes him feel unclean. Salt grease stuck to his hair. He wonders: *Have I done something wrong?*

The foghorns are blowing out the steamers who have come too close to shore. The park may close early this year. It was a bad season for the dogfish. The island is moving further out, floating into a gray line scraped out between the ocean and the sky. M can see where the currents are taking them. They are the last rock before the horizon. Alone now, he will be pushed all the way across to another side.

With her last words, she said to him, *the skin we wear is all we have.*

His father stomps out, letting the bedroom door thrash open. On the mattress, only an imprint of a body remains in her pale blanket, the one with a watery sunset dyed in cotton. Now, these faded clouds are disrupted with sickness and torn stitches of his mother's skin, like moth wings that M takes in his palm and blows out the open window.

He sits there until his father returns, and when the man aligns himself beside his son on the floor, he says nothing, takes a red apple from his pocket and sucks on the skin, breathing through his nose. The two of them stare into the rising, morning light and share the apple, bite for bite. The hair of their forearms mingles for the first time, close enough for M to see the sun burned into his father's skin, and a set of raised freckles shaped like a certain constellation which the mother always traced on his own twig of an arm.

Dear M,

I wrote a love letter once and pressed it to my chest and then pressed my naked chest to the wet cliffs not far from your home. I think you know what this feels like. When you reply to this letter, and I hope you do, please tell me how naked you feel right now, like you've been turned inside out and there're boot prints in the lining of your skin. I'm not making much progress. Tell the truth, M. Does it really hurt so bad or do you sometimes like it and invent the pain?

New Englanders can be so damn resigned to the long haul. What is it with all that sadness? What's that layer you have wrapped about you? So shy and proud on some secret path only you know, through the channel of an infuriating spirituality. Naturalism. Bullshit and a beer served cold. Does that make you uncomfortable?

You have no great monsters haunting you. You only have the means that I give you to scrape the bark off your own origins.

I just yanked a hangnail and it is bleeding more than I expected it to.

I was watching a beetle walk across my blanket this afternoon and I thought of you. It had a strand of black thread caught on its back leg, a hair. And the hair seemed to stretch forever, but there was nothing attached to the other end. I want to think our histories do not determine who we become. People in charge, they try to make us all look the same so our failures and their judgements can fall with the same hammer, but it doesn't work like that. I still want to tie something to the end of that hair, even if you've lost interest in my memory.

I'm trying to make you smile through a window. It is not enough, not nearly enough and I'm sorry. We must keep trying.

Yours truly,

INCARNATION RISING

There is one speech that M's father gave him, which remains stuck to the ribs. One brief story that haunts the pages of M's curiosity, sinking into the empty spaces, alighting the deep water of nighttime. A story which was perhaps intended to shrink M's mythic ideas of exploration, keep him close, keep him plowing down instead of forward, but ultimately had the opposite effect.

I dunno what your mother told you. A group of young, back breaking men settled this place to rid themselves of the legal binds of this growing state among the new united. This was not so long ago as to be dropped from the memories of those old guys who play cards down at the dock, who scoffed when M's father brought his mother out by marriage. These men flutter their hands and flick their burning cigarettes when they see M drag his feet down the road.

Don't you mind their little cock club. They will fade away just like their bullshit sailor tattoos. Anchors away. Right and so, little by little more people arrived with nothing but themselves to share. People of labor and tide, who would bail you out as soon as throw you overboard if the lifeboat was full. This is not your mother's story, boy. Don't look so damned unsure, it will always get worse before you find out the truth and you'll never find out the truth, so just listen. All's you can do.

There's one man would come and go, a guy the rest stayed clear of if they could help it. Rumors flew like mud round the Captain. He owned his boat; took pride in everything he stole. Broke every damn law in the books. He robbed all right. He hurt people. He raped, murdered for money or a woman or just to prove he could. He had this sly look about him, a long beard, sharp black eyes and tobacco teeth that pointed inward, like this. His father made a wedge with his hands, pointing toward his own chest. *That's how you really know you can't trust a man.*

The Captain had a crew that came and went and took whatever too, mostly he kicked 'em to the curb when they got to talking too much or coiled the rope wrong, a real stickler to get your shit right or get your shit dead. They say his palms were always raw from holding onto any damn thing he pleased too tight. Real obsessive. He could crush you easy as a can, if he wanted. He made a lot of money around these islands, more than we'll ever see for damn sure and laughed the whole time doin' it.

M had never seen such pleasure on his father's face. A look of admiration, respect even, the kind that lulls sailors to lost graves. These myths separate the island from all other places and tie his people to the lantern signals and water currents that carry them further and further out. Perhaps his father wants to hurt something like the Captain hurt things, his feet won't hold still and the mother's flame is suddenly bright in his father's almond shaped eyes. M finds himself stuck, craving the roughness of his father's voice. The father uses each pause to breathe loudly, making juicy smacking sounds from the back of his throat, as if hoping to lure the bats swerving above their heads. A story like this makes the island's people essential to their own reality. This is the only way that his father might ever feel real.

This captain, he liked the dirt to stick underneath his fingernails but didn't waste time lookin' up at the damn full moon, let me tell you.

Not a chance, kid.

The point is he made a lot of money back then, off cargo ships or passenger liners or anything with a purse on board. When he was finally ready to retire, he chose this rock because, as you know damn well, we're the furthest fucking out. The people that was out here kept to themselves, or at least turned the blind eye. They'd save their gossip for under the covers, once the doors were locked, same as they do now. His loot is still buried here somewhere, sunk to the bottom of them marshes I suppose, or maybe dug up in those woods.

This place can't be anything but what it is, not without dying first. And not a single person wants to deal with the grease stain that death leaves behind, not a one. So, we all just keep goin' same as we always knew how.

Places leave stains too, kid. Places are not so different from people. A home is a home.

Makin' it the only way we know how.

HUNTING FOR WILD

His father wandered off, taking wide steps toward the shed where the broken traps are always stacked, waiting for repair. He refuses to use the wire crates that don't break so easy, preferring to mend holes in the netting by weaving slowly with a hook the size of a bigger man's finger. The cotton rope rips easy but it holds his fingerprints longer. M imagines his father and mother sitting, sewing beside one another with their feet in puddles of gas, stabbing at each other with the cold lick of their divergent stories. M points his nose toward a hot wink in the distance, speaking beyond the lighthouse, into the dark.

M: Did you ever think the blood inside your tongue was poison? [Takes the grass between his toes and pulls up hard enough to make a ripping sound]

Captain: I don't care if what I do hurts anyone so why should my insides hurt me? I like the taste of iron though. Look at you with your cock and balls in your hand, you idle shit. What if I put my sharp knife here in your palm and pulled?

M: I have no feelings for you, and yet I dream about you. Your ship comes up to this shore and you take me away in a locked chest. Where did you hide all that treasure?

Captain: Enough with the questions. Sure, I'll take you out to sea. Don't you want to float away? Now that whore's gone and left you. Your mother was a useless kind of woman. We need more like her. Now dig deep, son. Forget her cheekbones and wool skirts. Forget the bullets of her hips and full shoulders that spelled grace backwards. It's not her you are talking to. We're all you've got now. [Yanks his beard and a dead moth falls out]

M: I want to smell her hair. I want her to fight with my father over the grocery bill and tie him to the bedpost and then hum again in the morning while she makes black coffee in the dirty pot. She can't be dust. She's not allowed to be. Where have you put her?

Captain: Fuck you, her cunt I don't dare touch, not even if the North Star took a nap on my back. I have no treasure hidden here. [Knocks a hard fist on the cliff above M, then swats a mosquito away from his eyebrow] What do I got? [Shoves his hands in his pockets and pulls out lint and a burnt match] Well, I got love letters written by hand, sewed into the lining of a rib cage made of spruce, wrapped with heron's wings and secured to the bottom of this damn island so hard that your little paws sure as shit won't pull 'em free. Seek and you shall find.

M: [Talking down to his own crotch, which has already grown a long curl of a cow lick across the pubic bone] You think I don't know how to write the word love. I'll find my own treasure.

Captain: Well then, an attitude. Send a letter to your damned mother, if you must. Drop it in a bottle and lick the cork. Toss it and be done with her, with all women, with everyone. Set fire to where it falls in the tide so I know how to follow it out. I will make sure it drowns safely.

M: Fine. Who needs some tired, old man to tell me the right way to get what I want? I have her. I always had her. She just left before me is all. [Yanks bits of a thumbnail off with his two front teeth and winces while doing it] I don't need your treasure or your love or your bullshit. I'll be gone soon enough. [Spits thumbnail bits into the captain's beard]

Drums beat from inside the rock that surrounds them as the Captain presses his palm into the back of M's head, and points to the heaving sea. Up and down. His lips are moving, but M either can't hear or is not listening anymore. The coastline is flat tonight. A solid, black stomach into which M's story is swallowed. Bucking backward so that the Captain's hand falls limp to the ground, M uses his hands to hoist himself up from the warm, muddied grass. His boots dig small ditches in the wetness. Disgusted, he moves silently past the shed and his undone father.

SHE INCARNATE SET FIRE TO

His father sleeps in the shed that night, in his high-water boots. M sleeps in his mother's bed at the end of the hall. He has this dream:

A crooked house, high and tumbling over itself. All the shutters are open through which a strange guest approaches. She can see through, to everything on the inside. Everything is in one small room: the toilet, kitchen sink, a closet door torn off its hinges. A mirror tall and thin stands empty at the end of the hall and another mirror above a shabby dressing table reflects the angle of her sharpening profile. She has dark hair sprouting from her armpits. Eyebrows the same color. It all fans out, away from her. Crow's feathers. Long, tight arms that have shed their weight and float up. Her body is hard everywhere else, except the eyes. The eyes seem stunned in pain. Her skin glows red just below the neck, along her collarbones, as if she comes from a bath of boiling water. She is emptied from a pot on the stove. She burns so hot. The glow exposes secrets, tugs at M's thighs. There is nowhere he can hide from her.

He senses that he has grown older. His hair is longer at the top, blown back and weighted with its own sweat. He can tell that he has done many things outside of this house, but has returned to its rusted locks and will never escape again. He senses new knowledge, answers to things asked in a letter, sealed with spit and buried deep, but only silence comes from his mouth. No tongue. No teeth. He feels wet, hungry, and open between his legs. He might be laughing, but there's no sound.

The shutters need to be closed. M does not want to be seen. She'll be able to walk through the open door soon. The kitchen sink is running, a deadening trickle of rusty water.

There is a black bull standing on the kitchen table. Its weight bends the wooden legs. He is young with small, tight testicles, and red eyelids that flutter against the sand filled wind, now blowing through. The bull is stuffed with raw cotton, filled with fake muscle and wax blood.

M mangles his own body, starting at the middle, ripping and tearing. She is coming inside. The only thing he can focus on: the hard, small horns budding from the skull of this bull specimen. Sweat and milk slide from the now prone creases of M's crotch, afraid to turn his back on the yellow anger of the bull. The animal wears the flattened, black fur coat that his mother kept wrapped in plastic at the back of her closet. She would slip it on in secret, naked underneath, when his father was out fishing overnight. He always returned from these trips none the wiser with a moist and raw nose. A nose that looked very much like the one stapled to the stuffed body of the bull calf. At least it appears so. He'd have to move closer to the table, closer to her and to the animal, to really see.

Dear M,

I was imagining a pleasant conversation we might have some day, but I started to fall asleep and jerked awake only when this red spider crawled across the inside of my wrist. I don't know what that means, but I won't let it be something bad. I don't think the spider bit me, but I smelled your mother's coffee anyway and was brought back to the island full steam.

How might I go about staying anonymous? Is anonymity the same as hiding? I do not want to be called a coward, but I stare into the corner of the room and I scare myself. I taste rotten fruit at the back of my mouth and I see shadows in the open doorway. No, I'm not afraid of you. You empower me. You give me the excuses I need. You are the purest of privilege and we all like to imagine what that must be like.

I've been sleeping better, imagining how I might tear you apart with words. Cut off the excess, the unnecessary. I'm going to steal your love from whatever rock it is hiding beneath and make you better at loving by writing you a better story.

I've been taking more naps this winter, afraid to leave the house and I imagine the sound of your breathing beside me. Have you ever deprived yourself of anything? Will you ever be denied?

Suppose you could live forever on the rolling tongues of your biggest fans. In a chorus, they all seem to approve of how fast you are growing.

Yours truly,

A BONE'S EDGE

M's father has expanded in the space they share, inviting him closer to the stove, watching his moon-pale face a little more closely, sharing the wash bin after dinner, trusting M to rinse out the bait barrels.

It is dusk in August. M is sloshing the thick, bloody water round the bottom of the last barrel when he hears a couple of dogs fighting not too far away. M has grown fast, now near his father's height. The scent of salty death lingers on his skin at age sixteen. Hormones and oil. The splintering fish bones get stuck in his calluses now, but he doesn't feel it. These new similarities keep his father from chasing him into the surf. He has begun to notice that people look at him longer, perhaps unsure who he is, father or son.

When the sudden noises crack off the shed walls, M drops his hose and takes four heavy strides out the wide door. He doesn't pause to turn the water off at the spigot. He walks briskly toward the barking. He hears loud slobbering and perhaps the low echo of bleeding. He had a dog once, which refused to eat after his mother died, and finally chewed through its rope late one night and disappeared. Its shit had long rotted, leaving dead spots in the grass.

Over grown branches reach into the path and stick to M's thin shirt as he strides toward the road, little pulls in the knit, not slowing him down just popping off and quivering in response to his curious speed. He doesn't feel prepared to assist in whatever situation he may come upon, but needs the information, needs to pack up the image, store it away for a winter memory. He wants to be present for everything, just to watch and wait for a collapse or for a well to spring.

The path seems particularly long, stretching before him on its own horizon. His steps are silent, but the barking ahead of him grows in desperation.

At the lip of the road, two dogs are circling an old man, slicing the air raw with their noise. He seems trapped, standing but paralyzed, as the dogs dance around him, white spit flying as if from a split artery.

It's Sam, another fisherman, long gone blind with age and the sun bouncing off ocean. Sam has nowhere to go and M doesn't move either, not forward to help or back toward the house. As M stares with a tensed jaw, his father pauses to his right, out of breath. He must have heard the same noises and taken the path leading up from the water. His father's hands are soaked in black engine oil and his sweaty eyebrows bush out like caterpillars beaded with morning dew.

These dogs want each other's throats. M recognizes one as his own, but the bastard has changed. Ribs exposed, patches of black fur pulled from raw skin, teeth brown with blood. The animal has bitten his own tongue and quenches his thirst with it. The whites of its drooping eyes are red now, swollen and watery. The other dog seems to stand erect and M notices its gray penis exposed from a sheath of thick fur. They would have already torn at each other if not for the man caught in the cross fire, walking home perhaps from the bar or the post office. M stands with his feet wide apart and has stopped breathing.

His father does not hesitate a second longer, lunging forward with the balls of his flat feet, and throwing his arms out as if approaching the man for a hug. M has never seen his father hug anyone. His hands shaped like claws, he turns with a strange stiffness and throws a shoulder into Sam's gut. Sam's lungs empty, heaving a choked sound into the space between the five of them.

The dogs swallow the air without pause and use the shifting bodies to launch into each other. A slap and crack of bone. Sam is tossed into the ditch on the east side of the road. M's ear catches a ripping sound that must be fabric, Sam's ratty pants against the dry dirt, which is coarser along the edge of the road.

The dogs can't resist the surge of their bodies slamming into each other. M's father expands again to collar their necks with both hands, spread wide and tense at the wrist. He slips on the dirt and falls to his knees, where the position is easier to wrestle the dogs down, but his chest is now eye level, splattered with blood from the ripped mouths of the animals and black oil from his greased-up hands. The fluids, from muscle and machine, splash in parallel arcs through the frozen air and bead in the dust of the fight.

M stands there, the machine within him not quite able to act. He waits with a spectator's expectation that this will end quickly enough.

M's father makes a sound he has never made before in the presence of his son, a rattle of the throat. It echoes to the water; an aged fire siren, awake at first than resigned as it fades back into his chest. It is the sound of pain before pain starts. He is lying on the ground now, tangled in legs and fur. The jaw of the dog that M used to feed from his own plate is clamped tight on his father's armpit, a shepherd's mouth wide enough to reach around the left shoulder, gripping both tendon and bone. The dog pulls back to defend himself against the larger dog that is oblivious to his father's body. M takes one step closer to confirm his suspicion that the hair on the back of his father's neck is raised. His shoulder blades protrude and his spine is bent, exposed, as if it is about to extract itself from his skin and slit the throats of each animal in turn.

The ease with which the dog's teeth rip the meat off his father's muscle strikes M as oddly comforting. Its eyes crisscross toward the wound and dilate, as if aware of the mistaken target but unable to correct it. This makes M smile round the corners of his mouth, before he has a chance to realize the crookedness of this response. Sam appears to be sitting up in the blurry background, staring through the fight, straight into M. Still, M is the only credible witness. Sam cannot see his passivity, unable to judge the insensitive up turn of his damp lips. Until this moment, it's possible that M thought his father was made of metal, of fishing hooks and impossibly tight knots.

M gets away with his stillness.

The spectacle does not last long now. Sam begins pelting rocks the size of ball bearings at the noise ahead of him, missing only narrowly. M's father raises a sweaty arm, drops his fist, bigger than a softball, to the dog's temple. The dog's jaw rattles audibly and remnants of his father's body slide off his bloody tongue. The dog cries out, a sound that is shaped like his mother. It jumps over the fallen father, jetting into the trees. The other dog rears back to follow, but hears an approaching truck down the way. Its legs carry it into the ditch not far from Sam. Just then, Sam cocks his throwing arm back, turns to his left and launches a final bullet at the rustle of leaves. This time he strikes, a direct hit, exploding the dog's naked eye, forcing the animal back into the woods behind the schoolhouse. All this in a kind of strange and remarkable quiet.

COOKING GOOSE BUMPS

On the night M's father dies, M serves him broth boiled on the stove while still in the can, which he sliced his thumb on. He has never watched his father eat. The man is shaking, sweating through his mother's sheets, into the mattress underneath. M sits on the edge of the bed, holding up a quivering tray with the steaming can, a glass of water, a paper napkin folded into a rectangle and damp with the drips off his father's ragged beard.

It is now that M realizes his mother's scarred leather suitcase is gone. Most of her dresses, long drapes of scratchy stitches, gone. Her dresses were made of a million pine needles, sewn together tightly. Only the light scent of cedar and mothballs fills her now empty closet. Even the fur coat is gone. The chest of drawers is at a crooked angle and looks as if it were charred by fire.

On the night M's father dies, he eats four spoonful of chicken broth and does not feel the burns on his tongue. His reddening eyes close. His eyelashes paint the pillowcase with yellow infection. The bandage is soaked through. Traces of the black oil remain, his skin singed with the goo at its ripped edges.

M lays down on his stomach, close, beside the body. His father slides a heavy, right palm to the base of his son's shirtless spine. For the first time the father touches the son, skin to skin. M rests with the pressure of this touch on his hollow vertebras. They both sleep shallow.

Just before sunrise, M wakes up to the sound of seawater boiling. His father's eyes are wide and dry, staring into M's open mouth.

LIGHT MACHINES, OUR CAPITAL

The sounds of summer dry up by the end of September, winter is closer than anyone cares to remember. The continuous breeze drops to a quiet lull. Chains clatter at the north end, where the park is beginning to cover its machinery, locking it tight from the salt spray of November. The colors have faded, mold clusters at the seams of each plywood panel, but still: pink elephants flaunt their rear ends on miniature rides, two-dimensional beach ball jugglers shake their shoulders around the Ferris wheel; all toxic green, unnatural cerulean. Golden canaries fly on wires overhead and flatten under foot, accordion echoes from the fortuneteller booth. Frivolous promises dished out of decadent silver bowls from supposed faraway lands. These tapestries of forget trace the water's edge. Money jars emptied. Everyone will leave soon.

A persistent trill of coins and the rip of randomly numbered tickets makes M lustful, even jealous of the retired tycoon and his persistent flow of cash. Until the last coin falls, he calls to the tourists and sailors, mothers and babes, *Come to my fair hideaway. This once in a lifetime experience, playground for the rich and the poor, young and old. Paint your face. You can escape to the Shangri-La of New England respite. Sweet temptations this way.* $2. $4. $5. $10. Endless price tags for the rotting blossoms of each crooked grin.

Milky light glows at the center of the park, reflecting the dirty metal shine of another season stowing itself away. M's father died at the end of the month, with debt stuck in the cuffs of his pants. M cannot keep up with the boat maintenance and he is a lousy fisherman. Everybody knows it. The men his father knew best stare at him, heavy lidded, and spit after he walks by. They hate him because he is not interested in their daughters; child thirsty, loitering around the wealthy summer boys who work the most popular rides.

None of the rich boys have calluses on their palms. None of them stink like M, breathe shallow like him, know the sound of a tide leaving port. And this makes him curious in a worthless kind of way. They hate him because they know he will leave.

M walks by the small bay where a mock pirate ship creaks, releasing a tired sound, a decades long snore.

He relishes the walk down the quieting pier; every memory, every story and song, all those conversations with the dead. He reaches for the rope that docks the Captain's play ship. It seems to mock his debt. To capture the vessel would be a joy. To lock his body in the hull, let the first fall storm pull him down with the snails. He'd happily be dessert for them, at the rocky bottom. But he keeps walking through the playground and it shrinks tight around him.

When he returns to his father's house, a decision has been made. The light is dripping now below the framed windows cut out of stone. The glass shows no reflection as he enters, only a winking, a smudge of remaining daylight eclipsed by an impending moon. The wooden chime tied up on the corner of the house is unmoving, wordless, put to sleep by the dampening heat of the evening.

His mother is gone. His father's body has gone to feed. There are no instructions and no person he cares to rely on. Seventeen years old. Translucent skin, burnt pink at the edges of his large ears and bulging nose. His clothes are thinning. The islanders have started taking their flags down earlier and earlier as dusk peels back across the landscape.

SEA CHANGING

M sits at the nail and drift wood grave he built for the dog that killed his father. He found the carcass, collecting earwigs and creamy maggots the size and crescent shape of his own weak fingernails, while walking in the woods behind his neighbor's barn. Its wounds were more severe than M could recall. The neck and left ear ripped open and infection sealed inside by dried blood. Wide smears of oil flanked both sides of its body. M buried it in a shallow grave and staked the spot so that he could return some day. M buries his feet in the still soft dirt, talks down, into this spot.

M: You came here from god knows where, bought land in a secret deal and built a pyramid to yourself, to your own fantasy. [Turns an accusing look toward a fat shadow stuck inside a blackberry bush]

Tycoon: I was bored. I was finished scraping the land I was born to. The earth is so rich here, so old, but untouched. No one seemed that interested in saving it from me. You make out like I'm some harlot, some land pimp. I just see an opportunity and take it. Capitalism, my boy.

M: The land you starved, the land you left, I think I might go there. I'm looking for something too. No one ever thinks to ask if I'm ok. It's as if I'm already gone.

Tycoon: The desert I came from is tired, but maybe you'll find what you're looking for. Doubt it. I have to ask, son; you ever had a woman? [Spits tobacco juice, a color M has never seen, onto the grave and M flinches] You ever wanted a man, faggot? [He grabs his crotch and shivers]

M: The lugworms like to climb up my leg. Sometimes I let them bite me. [Gestures to pull up the ripped cuff of his shorts, but stops short]

Tycoon: Well, isn't that somethin' sick. I never heard that one before. What, am I your priest now? I should charge for this.

M: I like how it stings.

Tycoon: Not sure what strange root you crawled out from under, but I like you. You got the look that says you can't keep those legs still. Keep moving with your mouth open, take a big bite and chew good, that's all you have to do. Seize the god damn day.

M: What really brought you here? Why stay here? Why build a dream in our backyard fit for the cold side of hell?

Tycoon: I don't have to explain myself to you. This whole damn island is just a study in broken mirrors, son. You should know that better than anyone. Can't you feel it? Got that vine wrapped around your waist so tight, you're afraid you might drown if you cut loose. Get the fuck out of here. It's good and time. You're starting to smell like fish rot.

M: But what do you know, really? If you want to erase us so bad, why not get it over with? I want what you have so bad I get sick, stupid even. You're so blind, just looking right through things and yet you thrive. How come you get to be so free?

Tycoon: I suppose, it's because I'm just an abstraction of flowers in another man's lapel. I'm not really here. Shit, wouldn't be caught dead on this god forsaken island. All you need to see is money fruit falling from my branches. [Shakes his arms out wide and loose more like a scarecrow than a tree and M feels the acid of jealousy in his gut] Nobody thinks to ask me what I'm really feeling. Why should I give you that courtesy?

M: [Feels heat from behind his belly button, spreading, pouring out into the damp night. Steam rising from the plans he is drawing out in the dirt, in the code his mother taught him]

Tycoon: Tell you what, if you don't leave now you ain't ever gonna have more than this one shit-house story. It's gotta be about you now. Here on out, you and only you. Get gone.

THE NERVOUS SYSTEM STARTS IN THE HEART

There are toothless men on the island who seek M out. He walks silently down the night road. He has just watched the park shut down, the kids squeak their rusty bikes toward home or a secret elsewhere. It is high tide. There are more decisions to make. Down the south point, where the constable doesn't go anymore, M watches a few curtains open at the corners revealing the addled men inside. Their wives, their amply organed women, have either expired or abandoned them on account of their weak pricks and the poison their veins lay prone to.

Most nights, M slowly nods his head and sinks deeper into his walk. These gestures, the signs they make in the window do not necessarily encourage him to their cheap companionship, but imagining what it must smell like in those rooms brings an odd joy. He smiles at their kindness, at the intimacy they perform, touching themselves just for him, laced with a small stinging threat. He will miss these men and their caves of escape. There are decisions to make and these last nights on the island have no room for any more distractions.

These nights have been happening more frequently, in anticipation of M's quiet disappearance. He cracks through the worn latches of summer basements and steals the copper piping within. What little money it may trick out at the mainland salvage yard will get him between here and somewhere. No one will know otherwise until the basements flood next June. These houses are closed up for now. The whole place is shutting down.

Adjusting to the added darkness of cold, stone walls, M fingers the jagged edge of cut metal, sawed through with his father's blade. It burns a little. The touch makes his back teeth go cold and his jaw cramp.

He has been hiding his stash in a beached dingy with splintered holes in the bow. The boat's christened name is Delilah, in red cursive along the stern. M has been watching the pile of metal grow, hugging itself in her belly. Tonight, he sleeps with the stack so he won't hear his father's body moving through the house, or his mother's voice in her abandoned wind chime.

In the early morning, he melts tar in a coffee can and patches the holes in Delilah, the escape vessel. He takes the old oars down from the wall of his father's shed. He shucks mussels for breakfast, uses the hot coals piled with seaweed to cook them tough. He can smell bacon frying from somewhere down the way. He pulls his arm hair to keep warm against the brisk air.

It is time to move. Time to go west, to where he knows nothing, where the land is young and still swelling with that potential to become something new; no matter what the Tycoon wants him to believe. One more day for the boat to dry, a single afternoon to cross the sound in a calm tide. Sell what he can and board the train that only goes in one direction. The anticipation of this chance smells of turpentine and sun fried barnacles. The apples have already started turning red. M kisses his father's door as he locks it and hides the key under a triangle piece of slate beneath the stair. He packs no bags. He ties his leather boots, holes in each sole sealed with leftover tar.

Dear M,

You know I understand the impulse to leave this place the size of a teacup and you too tall already, so long and pale. Head scraping the ceiling, feet stuck in the sand. I can see your purple veins. Do you imagine yourself a sailor setting out to chart the wild sea?

I'm no genius. I'll probably never figure you out, but don't you dare over simplify what it means to have a body. Though I agree, it's never as good as it is in your head. What I'm trying to tell you isn't coming out right. You're so self-assured, aren't you? I'm proud of you for leaving, but nervous too. The first of many departures, keep your suitcases close.

I have a map I was going to give you. I changed my mind. I kept it for myself, stapled it to my groin and now I have to tilt my head at a funny angle to read where I'm going next. Or rather, where I'm going to take you.

Yours truly,

EVERY _____ YOU LEAVE WILL HAVE A TIGHTER MOUTH THAN THE NEXT ONE

M catches the train just in time, like the silent movies: a man clinging to the last rail on the last car, waving good bye to a passionate love or no one at all. He spends the bulk of his copper wage on a private cabin after watching a mother with three loud, wet children ushered into the economy car. One day gone to the tracks, he stops trying to measure the actual distance through which the train is carrying him. He seems to have invented a family to miss, romanticizing a back home that is a sun-soaked shadow of its reality. He wants to call this homesickness. It has not stopped raining since leaving the port, but the train coasts at such a speed that the windows can be left open and the upholstery remains dry.

He sinks into the rocking motion of rhythmic clacking, cold railings, and Turkish-style carpeting, worn to grey wood in the middle. The whole car smells of cigarettes and damp rose petals, blanketing each cabin with a not uncomfortable, stale bathroom stench. These rooms are tightly pushed against one another. The food is not so good. M is an ant, among other wordless ants, packed into a middle-class tube and spit out of a straw, from one colony to another. M has no real thoughts of consequence to record and so stares out the window, watching the familiar shades of green and blue fade behind him.

He is beginning to feel like compost for the garden, turned over and over again, letting his heat escape and bacteria absorb. Fertilizer for a stranger's growth desperate to consume his body. The greedy rain speeds up this process.

M seems to live in his dreams; refusing to talk to people he continuously passes in the hall. He jots notes in code on cocktail napkins, denying explanation. Every night, he sleeps early and hard, tucking these codes in bed with him, forming a single dream: Water boiling on a wood stove, in a rusty iron pot. Faceless bodies wander in and out on the balls of their feet. Very tall men, hairless save for coarse curlicues at their cracks. Wide tracks of skin: white, tan, brown. Each man takes his turn sitting down in a wooden chair, pretending they have eyes to stare at M with from across the table. They tilt their heads, eerie and stiff, then a clock chimes, set to a time M cannot see. When one man stands, the next sits down, each taking turns to stand, then they bend over, stretching forward to place a large palm on the stovetop while mocking an intimate gaze to where M still sits. Smoke rises from the flesh on fire. The whole sequence begins again.

He wakes himself up indicted by the smell of burning skin. He can see shadowy shades of skin colored smoke dripping in shafts of passing light. Reluctantly, he pretends his eyes are sewn shut and falls back into the mechanism.

Burning stove. An iron pot. Faceless bodies, wandering in and out. A grid, straight lines, a cement floor. Very tall, hairless men walk on their toes, glisten with sweat. Hairless except for damp matting at the beginning of cracks, in the crests of lean chests. Limp dicks stuck to thighs. Each body moving in rhythm with the one before and the one after. Each takes his turn sitting across from M. Each blank face seems to believe. Believe it owns a pair of eyes with which to stare. Then like gears clicking in a timepiece, the stranger stands and another man takes his place. Then he stands and steps forward for the next one to take his place. Then one bends in half. His abdomen folds on top of itself and his crack exposes darker pigment, a shade of deep rose with a rotting bud at the middle.

M runs his hands down his thighs, which are rubbing against each other, making him pulse. A man is bent in half, to reach his palm flat on the surface of the hot stovetop. Steam rising, the way it does from the train when running away at full speed.

The smell of burning flesh wakes him up and he is convinced the train has crashed or breakfast has burned or a cigar has slipped from a lonely woman's lips. The carpet is in flames and singing the bottoms of the lady's tender feet. He can see shifting shades of skin colored smoke drifting through his cabin. He presses his heels down hard and takes three complete turns before digging his hips awkwardly into the mattress. He slips back into sleep with his mouth open. His face now intimate with the wall that connects him to the next cabin, thinking of the naked woman on the other side, hoping this will take him to a different dream.

SEA CHANGE

M rides the train to the end, as far west as the rails are laid. His clothes are starting to stink. The other passengers also tighten their bodies as they nudge past each other in the slim hallways. Arms straight to their sides, thick cloth of home blocking the skin also thick now with days of unwashed grime, sweat of the smoke stack, sweat of all those dreams.

Half way across the flat lands, M realizes he likes to travel, to move along a metal line. Leaning over the back rail the metal is hot, searing. Peeling black paint scratches his softening hands. This might be the first time he has not worked in so many days. These years of just surviving, working to keep a quiet house satisfied. His mother and father never asked for anything, work just happened. Nets to weave, roots to pull. The ocean makes you work before you know that you are allowed to say no. The ocean is long gone now and he couldn't be happier.

This afternoon the train began to slow, which starts small fires in his brain, wearing him out, thinking so fast. His thoughts are dry. Cracked lips. He hasn't spoken a word since last night, when asked by three different couples over watery cocktails, dinner, and then dessert: *What brings you out here, son?*

I'm joining my father.

I'm a writer.

I'm hunting for gold.

They each believed him in turn and the possibility of a true story stirred up a good taste in his mouth. He's learning fast. If his face tells a story, his tongue can act as eraser anytime he wants. He steals lifetimes he pretends to have already lived. He could feel the dull rock of the island leaving his legs. Opportunity wrung out over his shoulder, like warm water it runs down the trench of his back into his ass crack, down to the backs of his heels. He chews his food slowly, listening to the voices of strangers, and watching the leafless trees outside the window turn to ash in the dry dirt.

The voices he hears are louder now than ever before and give him courage.

Go on.

Go on.

Go on.

He spits on the blackened track, where the slime sizzles, then evaporates in seconds as if it never happened.

The sky forms a heavy box out here, filled with blank paper. It is not a circle of sand tightening around his ankles. M represents the invisible center of it all, a symbol and a person clipped to the page. He has not been drinking enough water. The vertigo is quick to come and go again. The box continues to get taller and taller the closer to the horizon the train seems to get. He reaches out his hand to feel the air shift as they heave forward. Within his right boot a toenail pulls at the thread of a dirty sock. The toe taps up and down, scratching the leather until the nail finally breaks off. A few thousand yards out, a flattened town appears. In the distance beyond: deep pocketed, purple thunder heads nuzzle up to scorched hills. It's possible rain is coming.

DIGGING IN

What pulled M here?

It is the opposite of everything else and a promise of nothing.

While disembarking, a few *good lucks*. After all, M is off to seek fortunes or else follow his father to a bed of worms. He waves a heavy hand, a kind of indefinite reply.

The lamps are being lit and churchy types retreat to their separate bedrooms. Where are all the young people? Only three wide roads run through town. The dust kicks up the cuffs of his pants. Down the main street, horses big as some of the buildings and a few wooden carriages here and there. The flop of each brave animal already turned to stone. There is no smell that M can pick out. He takes up the earth with his body and carries it down the avenue. Brown smoke rises and sinks into the cracks of his skin, sticks to his throat like remnants of a salt lick.

From the bottom of this shallow valley, those bruised clouds are crowding in above him, complimenting the distant wall of white-capped hills. He feels he's finally not alone, like this is what it could mean to never be forgotten.

He tells himself, there is hope in the decay of muscle out here. Sharp beaked scavengers leave little to negotiate with. Such inevitability. He likes the hardness. A resolute stasis. Every footfall lands on solid ground. The first time in his life he is not floating.

When something dies here the only things not eaten are fur and bone. M feels the relinquishing of his body and it is like coming out of a shell that's too small, willing to die. His mind is left to eviscerate inside the horses' salivating mouths. He steals a drink from a curbside trough. In his cupped hand the water tastes like clay.

Dear M,

The desert will take your virginity. You'll lose your body. Here it no longer matters, just currency for the voices in your head to spend on the night wind. I know what you're doing. Young man, you are mining for sweet water of the cactus flower.

I can hear the beat of your boots pounding a memory onto the page. Make your knuckles white, clinging so hard to this adventure, this spirit that will leave a testament behind.

As if I'll stay in bed just waiting for you, just waiting for your reply. My jealousy is showing like an exposed slip. My zipper is down.

Engaging in war begins with quiet words, you know. The kind of words that will be uttered soon. You will need to sign for the receipt of other people's bodies inside of your own. You will not starve. You will seal your commitment to future battles by what happens next.

Keep close these people of greatness that will shape who you become. The clowns, the scavengers, the statues of beauty, and ears to the ground.

Use us for all we are worth.

Yours truly,

WESTERN FLAME

Night falls fast and the desert swallows its own heat, leaving M underdressed. It begins to rain, cold and hard. With the darkness, every noise is steeped under a magnifying glass. M walks on, listening to porch conversations and the slight movements of nocturnal animals. Eyes and mouths watch him move down the road, he is lit by lamplight and they assess his worth by the sway of his hips.

Turning a corner, on the western end of town, he is met with a hill of a body resting on the steps of a hastily built church. A closer look: she is deep in thought, kneeling over a discarded mosaic cut out of glass, a rendering of the Virgin Mary, cracked down the middle. Only then, M notices that the church appears to have moved out, abandoning the virgin in the rain. Passing very slowly now, he considers if he might help her in some way. Seeking some personal benefit as much as a neighborly sacrifice.

Afraid to embrace her, or utter a word, he gets close enough to see her tears mingle with the rain. She lashes out a hand shaped like a bear's paw, grabbing hold of his loose pants, hoisting herself up. Her large breasts collapse into M's armpits with great force. Yet, she is polite and seems to recover quickly from her prayer. *Might I join you on this damp evening, lest my feet will freeze to the ground I seem presently stuck on*, she says. *A shame to waste such a lovely work of art. We'll come back. We will. Save her in the morning, I think.* Her breath, passing directly into his open mouth, is remarkably fresh and though soaking wet, she smells of a spicy perfume.

She swiftly takes control of their direction, leading him into a little square where a few gray leaves remain frozen to the desperate trees. She announces into his left ear that these frail fragments look very much like their elbows folded into each other. To M, everything has gone black and white. He is in the beginning of a film he's never seen, his nose the camera. His face afraid to speak its lines.

Let's fly away, you and I. She fidgets to fit better onto his lanky frame. *How fantastic, we'll forever be in the wrong scene.* She claps a thick arm around his back. Pushes her hand into his left shoulder blade, digging in and taking stock of his remaining clods of muscle.

They end up at a dimly lit bar, what M assumes to be a saloon, but she calls it a salon, a conversational pitstop before moving on to her apartments on the edge of town. M's nose follows her.

She ushers him into the blue flame of these windows as if she owns it, sits him down amongst several other limply clothed men. She so clearly approves of herself, her role of accepting and documenting their many secrets. She is a shining, tin butter knife ready to spread their fears thin. She buys everyone a round and a hot plate.

Everyone seems to know her metallic taste. In the light, her face is the color of a dying rose. His hunger is making it difficult to realize this opportunity. Only once does she graze the buttons coldly stuck to his crotch, seeming only to verify the as yet unused pieces of him she has already claimed.

Milky wine sloshes from a bottle tipped toward the counter by a sturdy pair of hands. The bartender claims: *Well is dried up again. Nothing but wine. Take a lick of that, will do the trick.* And the bulky man raises only his left hand as if looking for the better half of his prayer.

M's eyes are impossibly open, taking in the scene and rain still dripping off his ears. This woman wears a sack, heavily woven and loose threads catching on the wood of her chair, now leaking dirty water onto stained floorboards. The blanket of her garment may have filled a wheelbarrow or fit comfortably over the trunk of a young pine tree, roots and all. And she seems to love the dress, smoothing it over the rolls of her body, letting it stick in places and smiling at M all the while.

The young men around him are layered with grease, hair slicked to one side or the other. He begins to imagine, as she booms on about a day's worth of scenes with frank and sharp words, what these men smell like unbathed, in the cooking sun, what graces they might permit him. Would they let him scrub their bodies with sand and lick up the crust of crumbling sweat?

Their skin is dark citrine cut from starved muscle. These thoughts just arrive in M, too quickly to question and he taps out a cipher on the seam of his pants. He listens with a flat smile and sips his beverage. Buzzing now, he hopes real food is on its way.

Noticing the pressure of his hand on the table, the woman asks with persistent politeness, *Please, by all means, show me what you do.*

Since stepping onto the train, M's hands have done nothing. Was she looking for words, for some poetry to pour forth from him the way it seemed to from these men who crowd her in the same way that she knelt into him at the abandoned church? She rips a piece of paper from one man's notebook and rolls a pencil in his general direction, *what do you have to say for yourself?*

Nothing sifts through M, no confident marking up the page with brave stories. What he does write, no one understands and this brings a sturdy pleasure.

```
      .. -..-. .- / -- -..-. .- -..-. ..-. / .. / ... /
.... / . / .-. / -- / .- / -. / .----. / ... -..-. ...
/ --- / -.
```

```
      .. -..-. .... / .- / ...- / . -..-. -. / --- -..-.
-- / --- / -. / . / -.-
```

```
      .- / -. / -.. -..-. -. / --- -..-. / .--. / .-..
/ .- / -.-. / . -..-. - / --- -..-. ... / .-.. / . / .
/ .--.
```

A little embarrassed, he puts the pencil down as his hands start to cramp like when he fondles himself in the morning bath or when cracking the winter ice from the steps of his father's house. He wants to write about his mother sitting at the foot of his sand filled bed, but decides he's shared enough. The truth smells far less appealing now and the pencil's erasure fails him, he folds the paper in two while his audience makes gestures of silent laughter behind his back.

The woman unfolds her body in a slow way, squeezing swollen fingers into his ribs and wipes the sweat from his unwrinkled forehead with a fat thumb. She takes the dull pencil from his fidgeting hand and breaks it in two, dropping the pieces into her empty glass.

LOVE SCENE

Still raining, surges now sweep the street clean. Their mutually small feet rocking in and out of puddles that glow under the lamplight flames. They stumble from one side of the street to the other. The town is much bigger than M had first assumed. Men like long, soggy rats jump out, spitting questions at his companion, all of which she answers politely, confidently. Her round silhouette takes up all the space and pushes all the air out of town. She leads him to a large apartment with a high desert garden where two hairless dogs floss their teeth with the wire fence, fighting for her affection.

M stays with the woman, committing to the task of spinning their stories into new kinds of worship. They speak in variations of love, a kind of wistful family forming as their shoulders touch in bed at night. One story resting beside another story. He hesitantly grunts responses to her demands and receives herbal tea baths to soothe his sore throat.

The confident, yet forgetful, woman knows many meanings, although they are often of her own making. Her conversations are deep purple. Her marriage bed is hard with silver. There is a willingness to forget, yes, but also a son's sweetness in the dialogue bouncing off his tongue and into her sensuous, loud mouth.

M grows to care for her, wrapping himself around her leg, perpetually within and around her. And she, in turns, enters him.

She grows many plants that require drying out in the sun after the autumn rains. He tends to these children, as a cultivator might, enjoying the smell of chilled cucumbers released by the town, washed clean. Her home has windows as tall as his shoulders, always open to the portrait of their piece of land.

They fight vibrantly, laughing as much yelling. Reading out loud, side-eyeing each other while lounging outside, on iron chairs. She wedges her feet between his legs and together they let their coffees get cold.

Her rooms are richer and sturdier than any M have ever seen. Only the Tycoon's amusement park rivals her playful ignorance of money and space, the way she holds hostage an environment and the people within it. She enjoys velvet and a good echo, which only makes him feel lonely. He is frequently instructed to free the dust from all the drapes or lock all the doors so that she can ignore him, listening instead to the children playing in the alley, or the laundry flapping in clouds of desert sand just below their private rooms.

When M craves touch, he licks the used canvases which lay prone on her studio floor and waits until six o'clock light slants across their bed. His shrouded body soaks peacefully in the orange glow, naked beneath a sheet. She enters with force, ignores his fondling. Each time she releases a terrible sigh and sticks a few coins between his toes, telling him, *go out and seduce somebody.*

She has love affairs with the other architects of her social spaces and pinches the nipples of each of her partners to their hesitant delight. M envies her. Her solidness above all, the ability to own a room and its contents. He is such the opposite, still a wavering knot of vines and rope rolling out into the dirt, constantly stung by wind tunnels coming off the desert.

She demands that he create even if it becomes a lie. She is an artist by claim, though he never sees her work much. So, every day he sits at her generous desk writing out painfully long sequences of a code, taught to him by his mother in her time of war, repeating himself in patterns and rhythms that fill pages of thick paper and create a pattering sound like rain or ocean spray. And this just goes on and on. The desert does not change much.

Then, a young and foreign soldier arrives for dinner.

A SOLDERING

The soldier, this memento of recent violence still raw, wears rings with horses pressed into gold, horses in full stride. When they shake hands, it happens awkwardly, each so focused on the other's eyes that they nearly missed each other's grasp. The skin of this uniform is so warm. The metal of his rings, cold as late night. The stamp on his index finger left a red imprint in M's palm, which he traced onto paper once all the guests had left. So as not to forget.

First meetings make M quietly pine even if he's not interested in the other's signals and gestures. He likes to consume every bit of a guest before he resigns to open his mouth. On this night, he insists on sitting next to an infamous artist situating the soldier across from him at the table. So he can see just how the brave man might reveal himself. How does his mouth look when he finally utters M's name?

The next morning M wakes to the clashing of pots and pans in the kitchen and panics because he was sure the soldier was a shadow of a dream. But no, this uniformed bit of steel had left the scent of orange and clove on the front of M's shirt. He wanted to burn him, like incense, trap him in a glass box. M rests late into the morning, with his hands behind his head, staring toward the tiled ceiling through his shirt, pulled up and over his face. The soldier seemed comfortable, across the table, didn't he? Like they were old friends, who didn't need to speak to one another, just nip at the good brandy and accommodate their mistress's questions, light cigarettes for their neighbors. Upon rising, M quarrels with the cook about how loose his vest has become and in the midst of the kindly dispute he realizes it is time to leave.

But more days followed, he needed time to plan. It became more and more likely that M chose not to eat with the rest of the house. He would leave the table without a word to stare at the wall, repeating the man's name over and over again. Caressing the polished mahogany as if it was the soldier's precious skin. In doing so, he seemed to stretch preemptively across an ocean, sewing future memories into the lining of his jacket.

The hot season was fast approaching, the ground getting tighter again. Dry skin cannot be satisfied. His Madame, his wife, began obsessively putting on and taking off all of her jewelry. M was making a remarkable amount of noise now, stomping away from the red rings of her cheeks and the attempted seduction she would spin by holding her wine glass up to his. He soon stopped returning her ridiculous toasts. He recognized his own dislodging, but she refused to swallow the sound.

This outskirt of a town had become a scorched children's toy. He packed the pages filled with his obsessive ticks and slashes. He left behind all the things she had bought him, appropriated the contents of the safe and a string of her pearls that he always favored.

There will always be a secret between these two, hiding behind her body; the reason for arriving and staying at her table, to be fed, to be ushered onto a stage of pleasure and acceptance, to be indulgent in the deadest place he'd ever known, sweetened into whipped cream by the presence of someone who knows so much more and wants to teach, to transform.

M left the door open behind him, walking slowly back to the tracks that brought him here. He could already feel a new appetite dangling in front of his nose.

SAFE PASSAGE

A journey happens, again. M feels not the slightest twinge of regret from this, another wave breaking. Reminisces to himself about the antics of the little dogs, his mistress's hands, and their shared feather bed. He wants to call this homesickness. He moves fluidly station to station, a bit off balance but happy to be nearing the sea again. When he climbs aboard the steamship, his legs seem to right themselves, offering steadiness and renewed faith. The ocean wind lifts the dust from his clothes and carries it back towards her canvas.

The ship is a remnant of the war that happened above M's head. The world set aflame then pressed into ash and now rebuilding as if it could never happen again. He felt like he missed something, but couldn't say what. He didn't feel the singing of metal or have to choose, run or don't run. He'd seen photographs of boys in fatigues, had known a couple of those boys whose deaths had birthed heroic lives made into banner narratives, strung up island flagpoles. What he does know for sure: The rust on this ship looks like his father's wound, before the infection sunk too deep.

He retreats to silence again, watching the other passengers wretch over the side, their barely masticated meals of last night drowning in the impressive wake. He keeps writing, though without her hand to push his shoulder into it his heart questions the practice.

He has taken his mistress's name and this affords some premier access, which he celebrates with a constant cocktail hour, smoking finely rolled cigarettes while sitting in leather-backed chairs securely nailed to the thin carpeted floor. Legs crossed like a gentleman, he knows his mother would be terrified in her pride and his father would just laugh off the side of the ship.

A cool, blue cleat serves as his writing desk, in the afternoons when most passengers are napping. All that comes through him are the old patterns, all the same, cutting at a slant down the page. During one mid-day hour, an analyst rolls past, interrupting his sequence.

Your writing indicates that you come from the sea not the air. Your mind is in the depths not the universe. Yet, a code, I see. Interesting, indi-

cates logic. A precise calculation.

Sometimes the pattern changes as if on its own accord, but mostly the ticking rhythm beats through his fingers and spits onto the page, again and again. He thinks, he knows, the soldier will understand. This pleasant routine does not stop him from wondering whom his mistress has taken as her new companion. How long will she provide his allowance? In his left breast pocket, he fondles her pearls, resisting the urge to suck on them. In his right hand, the pen jabs obsessively.

Are there oceans where he is going? Geographically the world is set, but to M the whole expanse is so new, so faithfully unpredictable compared to the island, that birds can swim and fish speak in Morse. A man can be an artist in theory and have no practice. Any gesture he makes feels as though it is liable to kill the destination before he arrives, and this unknown is comforting somehow. M craves the risk, has faith in reward.

To be sure his mistress must regret teaching him all those pieces of language. He hovers over all her potential regrets, hoping she fears his absence, hoping she wishes she could apologize for degrading his desire. He feels reclaimed, recast in the warmth of Atlantic sun. He no longer hears her throaty claims of ownership and defiantly lowers his shirt so that his shoulders might take on some color, hoping to look healthy when he finds who he's looking for.

M writes and writes, letting his mind wrap around that handshake with the soldier, enjoying the breeze on his half-exposed nipples. He taps out each syllable with an unsteady hand.

.... / --- / .-.. / -.. / --- / -. -..-. .... /
--- / .-.. / -.. / --- / -. -..-. .. / .- / -- / -.-.
/ --- / -- / .. / -. / --. / ..-. / --- / .-. / -.-- /
--- / ..-

.... / --- / .-.. / -.. / --- / -. -..-. .... /
--- / .-.. / -.. / --- / -.

.. -..-. .- / -- -..-. -.-. / --- / -- / .. / -.
/ --.

.... / --- / .-.. / -.. / --- / -. -..-. .... /
--- / .-.. / -.. / --- / -.

Restless hands have to hold something or they go numb.

Hands rendered useless belong in the desert. He pauses only to eat a leftover biscuit. He leaves the crumbs in his chest hair. M's hands begin a new compulsion, twirling his fast-growing hair into fishermen knots. Couldn't resist, now he's hot and sucking on the pearls.

All of this observed by someone from just around the corner, someone who has been watching M for the length of the passage. Someone who has watched how M takes his morning coffee and removes his coat before he closes his cabin door. Someone's hand reaches from behind M's head and gently unties the noose that M has made in his dark blonde locks. The hand is large, smells like fish scales. M is pulled from his practice. He sits up straight, with the sun so blinding there is no way to orient the tease. Just a pair of legs leaning against his back, he senses a fine fabric wrinkling against his spine. The geography of their shared presence becomes unclear. M's pen bounces off his bent knee and the other man's foot kicks it into the depths.

TOUCH SCENE

[I've been watching you each morning, coffee black, picking only the stale biscuits. And you've been alone this whole time. We arrive tomorrow, care to join me this evening for a drink? A farewell to our floating retreat?]

The cabin door swings shut behind them, sighing like a cello bowed slowly. The sound of warming up before a performance. Through the walls, M can hear preparation for the night's festivities. The musicians tap their instrument strings and flirt with twittering maids. They are standing in a room connected to the great hall by floral wallpaper and metal. On the other side, where dinner is served, the other passengers serve as blind audience to what happens next.

M's Fingernail: Flicks open a button at the top of his vest.

His Hand: Slides to M's hip bone and stops along the edge of it, lingers, then loops a finger between his skin and waist band.

M's Fingers: Undo the fasteners one by one, shaking a bit, to touch the next layer. Linen. Just grazing the shirt makes M's pants pull. The lining of his vest is deep purple. Satin. M's fingers slide into his mouth to stop any sound, preferring to close his eyes and listen to the plates rattle above the comfortable laughter in the next room.

His Hand: Roughly now, unbuttons M's pants and pushes them to the floor, pushes M to the thin bed, covers M's face. The other hand takes hold of the cotton of M's undergarments and rips a wider hole at the front. Dives in to investigate, takes hold of M's hardness and explores the curly inches between holes.

M's Knee: Grinds into his inner thigh, rubbing as gently as possible, which is not very. Exploring the how far one can go.

His Hand: Pulls free from the trench, revealing between fingertips a small shred of paper. Wafts it in a circle around his nose and with his other hand opens M's eyes wide, holding the dirty tissue close so that he may see what he has excavated. M laughs uncomfortably. [Forgive me. I have not bathed in two days.]

His Tongue: Slides along the corner of M's mouth, tasting stale wheat and sugar. His hand hides the faint smelling remnant behind M's left ear.

M's Arms: Wrap tight around his waist. Pulling, squeezing air out of both bodies into open mouths. They mirror each other.

His Fingers: Pull at what's left of their clothing, gently and gracefully now.

M's Body: Is a flat slab. Melts across the bed. Turns over.

M's Nipples: Grow hard and red, but otherwise don't respond to his teeth.

His Limbs: Tangle with other limbs.

M's Tongue: Licks along his collarbone. Tastes sour traces of rich cologne, the way one's fingers taste after popping off the heads of dandelions.

His Feet: Manage to prod and stroke hard parts.

M's Spit: Works so well and flows so easy despite his rapid breathing. It serves just fine.

One Body: Thrusts.

The Other Body: Pushes back, harder.

And both finish again and again.

[Bene, che divertimento, my young friend. Un grande addio, bene,

bene. Sleep your sleep. I am hungry and shall retrieve some dinner for us weary travelers. Sleep your sleep. You are no one now, in my bed.]

The cabin door creaks open and shuts behind the man, now wearing a robe so richly spun with purple thread it appears black in the light from an open porthole. A spotlight. M watches his departure through the slits of his eyes, then turns himself to the wall further messing the damp sheets. His body is limp, wasted away, turned inside out and re-stitched with new openings. He bathes in the pleasure of that. He spreads his toes and fingers wide to feel their difference. He has shifted across a boundary and fallen into a restless dream in which his breasts are swollen and ready to be fed upon. In the dream, his sex still throbs in the varying folds he's just dug into. He becomes something glorious and other. Left wordless in someone else's bed. A newborn, again.

When next he wakes, the boat is tied to an impressive dock, sun spilt and splattered with a finely dressed audience who pretend to ignore his new form. He knows his body is now impressive. He is on the other side of an ocean.

Dear M,

I'm really loving this and hating myself for being the object removed. You have been swallowed by a womb, given holes that were not there before. Your heart makes a different sound. Even your eyes are a different color.

But still, you're letting others speak for you, through you. Still, I write you into a continuation of some pained existence, only now I've added coins to your purse. I'm trying my best not to erase you because I want your image to sustain its memory. The body lingers though our stories are made of sand.

When you wake up, you'll hear sirens. In the distance, the ringing of metal and grinding of bone will call you to a darkness, tinted with yellow, that will serve as backdrop for the best time of your life and this I would never erase, but I will make you remember it in a million different ways.

When this is all over, we shall know how to play with our bodies and which games produce the most pain.

Yours truly,

BOOK II.

MOURNING DOVE SING CITY

I first spotted M from the balcony of my apartment. I was wringing out stockings from the previous night and he was staring up at me, standing knee deep in a muddy hole where the new sewer line would eventually be buried. I recognized him quite quickly, the pale boy I dined with in the bright halo of the American west, but now, now he was drowning in shadow and shit. Only his face glowed from between my open legs. Perhaps the sun also shadowed me from behind. Perhaps he couldn't see me. My face, just a dark inkblot, a sunspot.

I was wrenching the cloudy water from this pair of stockings, as always too light for my skin, but the closest I would ever get, listening to a record that skips my recollection now. Perhaps I was smiling a headache away, a tight, thin smile at the thoughtless pleasure my friends always get from calling after me at dawn, *Yin-Yang, Yin-Yang, kiss me! Gute nacht, gute nacht.*

I caught him peeping in the late afternoon light, and recognized him by those long blue eyes and hands that can't hold still. Later, he admitted to admiring me even at this moment when he couldn't see that I was the one he was looking for. He loved that my body appeared to him as geometry; a simple triangle, carved and polished wood, upside down and my face invisible.

His sense of poetry came later.

That afternoon, all I saw was a ghost wrapped in cheap burlap, stuffed with dried herbs. I wanted to rip that calming scent out of him and make him into a bed. I recall one of my rings snagged the leg of the stockings and tore the cheap silk. I meant to chuck the wasted pair into the alley, but instead it feathered against the wind and clung to his shoulder. So, there it was: a talisman, the sign I needed. I invited him in for a cup of my strong coffee.

He came up the stairs slowly, with a young hesitation. I had ample time to make sure my trousers were buttoned but my shirt was not. What did I have to impress this kid for? Why was I suddenly buttoning my shirt back up, forcing my uniform sleeve to stick out of the open closet, scraping my makeup into the top drawer, blowing the glitter and eyelashes on the floor as if they were remnants left by a mourning dove's careless exit? You can never be sure who you're dealing with or how one might react to the unexpected.

Still several steps below my front door, he was no longer just a sad sack. Fragrant with his own dusky odor, yes, but up close he was more like paper, soaked in rain and then dried in a cellar. The strangeness of his gaze unnerved me but I took his hand and ushered him in whilst pulling my shirt cuff down, concealing the scars on my hands. Hapless scars, but silly to hide when all would be revealed too quickly.

We sat, me in my only chair, him on the corner of my bed, which was low and positioned his chest at the level of my hip. He always sat on the corner of things and I always take higher ground. He always rubbed at the hard seams of things and I always find the soft tear to stick my fingers in and pull.

He had coaxed my present location from his mistress. Said he thought he might love the romance of a post war scene and he needed to be free. He was anxious to stop talking about her and only wanted to know more of me. He had seeds he needed to bury and then add water, and then forget.

Mutual connections in Paris. A summer spent AWOL. *I was forced to fight. Would you like a café? Your madame became a dear confidante, advised me when I did not know where to go. She invited me to her desert, paid the way, insisted on back scratches and conversation that tickled my ears but I didn't mind. I had never been to your country before. I found it rather prudish and largely lackluster, and that's saying something,* as I look around my busted room.

Did I mind that he had intruded?

Into what – this reviled city? Grand gesture with both hands and arms. *It doesn't belong to me.*

Into my life. And I replied that life is a loose language here, to follow the law, or say your prayers, to set fire to a shot of whiskey and throw it in the face of the die hure who gave it to you or drink it yourself, it all amounts to the same here.

How many people have I killed?

Am I fonder of plants or dogs? The ocean or the desert?

I told him he was welcome to share my modest accommodations, but I would not tolerate judgment and a certain amount of pressure would be compulsory. He didn't understand at the time. The formalities clung to the dust in the air.

During our quiet conversation, the air had shifted, cold and flat. Winter seemed unable to let go that year. The evening still asked for a touch of fur around the collar, which I obliged by vigilantly scrounging the lice away from the stitched follicles of those pieces left behind by my mother. Hot air from the sewer-in-progress slipped through the curtain and tugged the base of my neck, sunk into my skin. The coffee revived my spirit. My face flushed; a rose dried beyond saving. This new toy made my purse feel fuller.

I proposed we celebrate his arrival properly by dressing up and taking an evening stroll, perhaps find a drink or two. I knew a place he might enjoy. He had brought little with him so I kicked that bag into the corner and opened my closet revealing not only more of the uniform but my best bonded corsets, white blouses with lipstick on the collar, two pairs of dungarees, a decent double-breasted trench coat, two red fox collars, splattered war boots, and a scratched pair of patent dancing shoes, among other things.

He started to loosen up after that. He seemed unafraid of my scars, which swirled up my arm and shoulder as I changed my shirt. When I reached for my comb, he reached out to me, as if to help, but he was just trying to touch the scars, to draw on them with tense, tapping fingers.

I had had so many kinds of toys in that old room. Since the war, since choices were made or made for me, I've taken in any melancholy les enfants de guerre as they have revealed themselves to me, but I have never had a doll of my own to play with, to dress up, to bend about. And now, one with such beautiful, budding breasts to admire so jealously. All night I felt as though I was on the balcony and he still far below, but I could wrap my hands around his face and lift him to my lips any time I wanted.

He seemed unable to play with words, but happy to twirl his hair in silence, following me two steps behind, listening to one set of marching orders then another. He asked questions which I narrowly ignored or answered in part. I pinched his elbows first and then his ass. His hesitancy made me feel more whole; I cannot say how or why, even now, I caught myself desiring him with an intensity that was deeply sad, like the feeling you get after you kill someone maybe. His strangeness seemed peaceful as an edible still life. I know now it was his violence that eluded me.

We dressed as proper, professional men. I even found a sailor cap for him and a crinkled top hat for me. I told him he needed to become *immolation incarnate*. He sat with his legs crossed at the knees and permitted me to draw the beauty mark, a large mole, to the right of a fine crease on his cheek, then I nipped at both sides of his face and his skin splotched red down to his chest.

Just a touch of eye pencil and a wool neck tie for me and we were out the door, leaving an uppity trumpet solo flying off the record in our wake.

One night not long into our courtship, I got thirsty for a little kissy face and ice cut straight off the block. Mix that with some sweet bubbles and easy fumes coming off the crowd and I knew I could be satisfied for the evening. M was tired of being dragged around, and then left waiting in front of a broom closet. Who could blame him? I tell him someone has to pay the bills. I've sold off all the war medals. Compensated myself by pressing them into my skin and once the imprint faded, I just took them off to pawn. *We have to eat more than the bedpost,* I say and give him a little slap across the cheek. He does not argue.

On the streets, I ease into a strut as if I'm always wearing my highest boot heels. I bounce. M drags, but I've taught him to quicken his pace in order to avoid the one-armed and hungry or worse, their wives.

Back on the streets, fliers and paper prayers stick to drainage ditches, crowding the gutters with pulpy sludge. I tell him, *the night doesn't have to hide anymore, darling.* The papers suggest new sanctuary, coating our streets with sweet, easy filth.

Come to us in Shangri-La.

Heal your wounds, Soldier, in the Basement of Beauty.

Discount for a friend, tonight only.

First show on us. Second show on you.

I warn M that the acrobatics of nighttime might leave us bloody, but what other way can we stop this machine from making exhaust of us all? He is always watching and it compels me to speak without pause. My voice grows hoarse from its own blabber. His voice grows hoarse from the dis-use, from his lack of ausspucken. I steer us towards the covert address. He always gets fidgety just before we enter, reaching for his missing cock and balls. I whisper into his collar: *They want you. They want you. Watch. Just watch.*

I reassure him with a pat on his flat ass and rap on the door:

Such shrines are for the faithful and we are among them! Nothing but finely spun gold here. And I will take care of you. Let's relieve you of your identity. Tonight, we'll load our guns and smoke them till they sizzle.

M lets everyone else get sloppy around him. He stands straight, dares me to touch my toes and I obey for that rare smile. We enter the show at half past midnight and the crowd has already started to glaze over, letting sweat streak their makeup. The blackened wall shows chips in the wood. A nail sticks out here or there, proudly displaying threads and sequins from so many snagged dresses. Dampened lamps are shaded in orange and rose. Round tables wobble as we pass, approaching the bar the polished floor creaks and I dig my heels in. The stage is set with thick curtains and a well-made chair, all of it pocked with cigarette burns that give the scene a volcanic impression. Large elephant palms line the wall, heavy with dust. The warmth feels tropical with bird's breath and a muslin of cigarette smoke whips by with each flick of hair or some other lustful gesture. The tin tiles behind the bar are hammered and dimple my face as I adjust my lariat and order an American whiskey, with ice. The stage lights rise in perfect sync with the parting curtain.

All I see are limbs. Such joy. A leg and a fractured arm with elbow skin a shade darker. Glowing. A tanned flesh colored tree waving silently in space, with vines, tight straps of cloth, tugging against gravity, growing up around this trunk. She is thick, but not large. Slabs of branches with very bony joints. Wide fingernails, chipped with red paint, and a pair of made up eyes. A stare that barks. The woman is sturdy, somehow still seeming to crumble with each muscle spasm, fighting against the air. She reaches to the audience, a look of desperate yearning. Calling attention to whom else, but M. I whisper: *They want you. Watch. They want you.*

And I want to see all of her but then start to feel like an object myself and hate them all for it. I admit that she chews on the tastiest morsel of every one of us here and we're so jealous. We know diese hure, Jemma the Gem. She opens her mouth with a set of full lungs to sing with but no sound comes out. She is yanked by a leash and a chain fused to her neck running into the hands of a young man. Ah Klaus, in a silk slip tonight, slit up to the crease in his hip. He sings on her behalf. His bra is stuffed but not so perfect as hers. The sweat around his nipples makes the tissue sulk. Klaus, un amateur parfaite.

She flexes her lips up and down and open and out. By the

bridge, they have switched roles. The spotlight turns orange, turns red. She swings a thick leg across the hollow stage, her long foot slipping just a little bit. She flattens her back above the young man. She wraps the chain through his mouth, a knee around his neck. Banished, tied to the chair, he opens his mouth. She sings with the force we so needed.

I love the taunt, but M looks rattled. The way her skin flickers as if I am staring at the sun through the trees on a car ride into the country. Wide eyes, made damaged with too much shade. She is ecstasy. She has worship on his ugly knees. I stare at her. The threat, the saint. I take my watch off and stick it in my pocket. A mother. A kid sister. *Tisk tisk tisk.* I am forever struck by the smell of our shared eternal history. Her flabby arms stretch across oceans. She fingers my vision, balances with me on the wood of a rotting dock at high tide. A vision I only know from M's stories. I shake my head at the mingling of worlds, the dreams of the man by my side and this evening's siren tears.

Her laugh is a rusty spring protruding from a piece of furniture you want to sit on really bad. She bounces. She pings out a secret code on your skin. I like it very much, and I wonder if M wants her too. She winks at the bar, that subtle demand for a drink.

The last time we came here, I got sloshed and M took me home. He whispered: *I want to draw your shiny boot in ink, send it back home, to die with me in old age. On my pillow. In my mouth. There's nothing you can do to stop me dying just like this.* Drunk as I was, I knew he thought I'd forget this by the next day. What he said. What he wants from me. I can't figure M out, so I fall prey to him all the more. He carries himself with a sensual disregard. He seems to teeter on the scale between a birth and a murder. This lures me deeper and I feel the need to take one strong finger, a living trigger, and rip open what's left of my skin for him.

I consider floating on stage, taking her body and choking him with it. Can his faith be so different than mine? Sturdier maybe, but so much less involved.

The smoke bends my mind in half, collapsing any understanding of whose body is whose. I can see the pulsing blood and tension around her neck. And mine pulled tight, needing to be filled. Her song is precisely timed, the length of a single cigarette. I flick the stub of mine onto the stage. M hands the Gem a drink containing small red fruits. Where did he find that ripeness? I haven't seen cherries like that since before the war.

She rips the pulp apart, juice running down those empty veins, puddling along her collarbones. She spits the little stem at our feet. A few tears, too, sliding back into her right ear. Klaus, the young partner extraordinaire, seizes her and *oh who will take us tonight? Herkommen. Herkommen.* Who will lick the tree's sap and spit her out onto the daylight street? Song and pain are tied together. She opens her mouth once more.

This time no one makes a sound.

In a corner booth, two women pause in their caresses to stare as the bodies on stage strangle each other. Jemma smiles at her finale. Twitching the wisps of her short hair in pleasure and turning her back to us. The fatso backstage closes the curtain early and it whips her powdered tush. Klaus steps out, alone, on the downbeat. He bows and lusts himself off stage to address his public. His palm slips behind my back and his fingers travel, underneath my boxer shorts, down the crease of my ass.

Busy night.

I can only think of M's fluids defying direction and consistency, cascading to the wrong places, all the wrong color. I eye his suspicion with caution and pleasure, thinking he might come right there, smelling of salt, but his tears are made of ammonia.

Klaus lifts M with one arm as if to rescue the man and my chance to push him too far is gone. I consider interrupting the women immersed in each other's mouths to ask for one of their black cigarettes, *Please Mesdemoiselles, for the love of our shared country.* My vision blurs and I move to the backstage of this scene, this scene of utter schatz.

Flying into such freedoms
feather plenty costumes empty
empty of blood

Forget the song through which we sing
Sliding off the bed back to the water
sink to the bottom
forget we promised you anything

Sirens call
Come play, come play
Everyone around you will disappear

Sirens, we swallow

Toughen up dear one
we'll suck your toes
We sense it's time to be disappearing
into silk robes of saffron rose and ochre

We weigh too much in your Dogtown
Our beds float on the crisp air high above this city
where we've already died and birthed new breast bones

Yes   yes   yes
We are talking to you and yours

I couldn't take his lingering anymore. I told him in German that I had forgotten how to speak English and refused to learn this silent language he was so eloquently speaking. I needed a night off. His allowance had just come in; he could find his own dinner. When I left the apartment, he was kneeling in front of my favorite chair, holding my shoe, and whispering a name I haven't heard in years, *Soldier. Soldier. Soldier, dear.*

It is easy for me to make weak tie friends. Faces licked with ample makeup, prisoners to plush booths or plywood stages. One might think the exploration would get tiring, but no, my bad dreams have turned me into a night hawk, sharp feathers and all. I devour these characters, these starving daughters and unemployed workmen. With shoulders unpowdered, these are men who think there's a king worth fighting for. These are women stripped of a vote, with mouths to feed, a god they can't stand, a bastard country. Some want to hate me terribly, then marvel at my true enough humanity. This is what I get for sticking around.

In honor of M's jackassery, I put on my uniform with the hope that it might bring some luck and lock the door behind me. I hadn't approached a woman in quite some time, but there she was. A sour faced hag with unbreakable collarbones and massive breasts. The rest of her frame looked like a square shelf built only for those bosoms to rest upon. She was on display, a stuffed bear skin on a rusty coat hanger. Beneath the netting of her shirt, fishbone tattoos etched across where her ribs might be. Her broad back was split with the weight of these darkly carved wings. I knew she would be uninterested in tickling my scars, but not every night has to be work.

She seemed like the type to deny a uniform. People often do in this kind of place. Katastrophe des Krieges. Her vacancy aroused my urgency. So, I had the bartender splash a healthy pour into her warm and empty glass. Then moved closer to her thick-skinned boundary. She was a lovely shade of rotten cream. Dark hair, slicked back along the jawbone, thick and hooked into her pores. I would know her forever, in this light and no other.

She did not unlock herself for me.

We spent the dwindling hours of Sunday, chatting quietly in accusing whispers, like tiny bullets. The hag thought my uniform was a fake. She thought I was trying to make a statement, something like *we should all want to forget*. We got quite drunk revisiting every last time we pissed on a man. I pretended M was not real. We lit each other's cigarettes.

The first time she slapped me it was to somehow prove that I was never a soldier. Her flabby triceps swayed on impact. I could feel the colors of a bruise climb up my cheekbone.

She said I smelled like her dead brother and asked, *Did I get you good enough or would you like another? Or would you mind, Herr Staatsmann, could you return the favor?* And perhaps too quickly I reciprocated. There, on a bench too small for the both of us, we birthed a blessing, a community service.

For two more hours, we took polite turns, alternating fleshy cheek, pound for pound. Our hands were nearly the same size. I had more blisters, which smoothed her raw. Hers had dirt dug into each palm but I didn't care in the least. Our slaps were quick embraces between two different kinds of veterans.

Our hands served as sweaty tongues in the swelling light.

She nearly broke the door in half when we emerged onto another stormy day. This woman. This force. Our cheeks were stained, a good deal swollen. Deep golden lines of parallel waves, her fingerprints rolled along the foundation of my jaw. She delivered a gentle kiss to the tip of my nose and I felt my country's emblem stitched anew into my heart, put together once again for however brief a time. We are worth fighting for.

I had been drinking water all night, by arrangement with the bartender, an old compatriot. My play was more successful than I ever could have hoped. It made me a bit sick to the stomach, the affair had been that sweet. She abandoned me then, bouncing down the alleyway, from wall to wall searching for an unlocked door. I returned to my little doghouse still wondering about the spoils of war, a finger poked through an old bullet hole at the loose waist of my coat. M was asleep with our last bottle of wine dripping in the crux of his elbow, empty. His eyes, half open.

I stood ready for a trap door to release me. For my body to be dropped into a canon and shot through him. Why did I take care of him? This way he had of steadily raising my blood to the skin, without a slap. What's that about?

I want to place him at the sensitive center of a target. I cannot deny his need for pleasure, or his lack of focus. He often looks through me as if I am someone else. Wandering abandon. His sleeping body hinted at needing to forget me. His arm twitched and he pawed at his own chest, whining softly. There are always ways to break a system from within. I knew, or convinced myself, that I would be as powerful as I needed to be.

Strangers, more loyal than me, will try to warn M about his self-fulfilling tragedy. If I were to pretend once more to be a proper soldier and kill him well, he still would not be satisfied. He'd rather listen to the chorus sing. He expects some kind of map to inform the way, but has no sense of direction. M is just the bones. The rest of us, all this good muscle, we will become the highest quality worm feed.

Since he arrived, my syllables have shadows. Each shadow has a sound, which M says reminds him of something else, something I could never understand. In this way, my syllables are starting to betray me. The sounds change, cut in half by light entering our bedroom. He won't leave. I draw myself to the attention of his hierarchy. And though our friends mock me with *Yin-Yang* for my mystic wonder and excellent balance and mixed skin, it is his symbols that will be trampled in the bloody mud.

A sharp breeze cuts his fineness. I am cross-eyed to the sky and my hair is lying flat in this moist spring air. Whispers of a new summer must arrive soon.

I've been documenting you too, I tell him.

He taps out:

-.-- / --- / ..- -..-. .-- / .. / .-.. / .-.. -..-
. .... / .- / ..- / -. / - -..-. -- / -.-- -..-. ..-.
/ ..- / - / ..- / .-. / .

A record so selfish I don't want to understand.

Eins: I've mastered how I shiver under his body, tailored it to match him and will tailor again to anyone in the future.

Zwei: These tremors I feel ricochet in my brain and slide down my spine, falling out of me from the roots. There is nothing greater for men like me. I am thankful, but do not say so. He tells me: *The nervous system starts in the heart.*

Drei: I will stay here until I can't stand him anymore.

She lifts a leg   shows all her sequins
Foot cramps   make it better
so much better

She thrusts   into wood
And splinters   an organ
a new cave

She delays   a beat
keeps time   in a glass box
for nights   like these

We dress in top hats   nipples for feeding
our hairless   bellies

garters beneath   the trousers we stole

We dress you in   patent leather dear
syncopate   knees
new tune   new trot

Soft landing. The two of us, together on the horizon of this lumpy, old bed. Metal frame rocking in tight circles. Our joints plow into one another, locked and hot with our weight. When I open my eyes, I witness our full range. A pulsing, just before we come, we see through shared eyes.

A shutter.

Wish we could take a photograph.

What color is the color of someone shining with love? Undergarments caught around alternate ankles. M's shorts match the fabric of the mattress now exposed by the sheet I've pulled tight, into my fist. Then I place him just so, knees bent. I bury my head, dig in. The straw pricks his pubic hair and gets stuck in his deep belly button. We break off into splinters of stuffing and frayed, damp thread.

He makes a noise I have not heard before, or since, as if vomiting me up. Out of his gut, I rise.

I see us from above, knotted.

One of the very good days.

I made some money last night, just for myself. Klaus had a friend who was visiting from a part of the country I had not heard of. He was lonely. I was on fire after an afternoon of play with M, who is finally beginning to blossom and breathe real air into those mannequin lungs. So pure, so dull, *sweet yang-kee child* and yet I can't get him out of my bed. I made some money last night preening the feathers of a tourist. All the mourning doves were jealous of my moves. I took him into their dressing room and laid him down on a chaise with worn leather trim. They opened their robes on the other side of the screen and licked their own curves with each other's fingertips. How I adore jealous birds.

Bodies I understand. M's body goes to battle with itself, and all that spiritual ceci et cela. It doesn't make sense to me. A war I can't win, or am perhaps sick of fighting. So, I didn't go home with my winnings. I walked the streets looking for something to buy. I climbed deeper into the well-oiled industry of the city, suspicious of its force. I am a civilian martyr, pennies in the pocket and wishes to make. This machine is made to grind bones. I walk alongside the spineless. The tank of the city still smells like fresh blood, though it has been emptying for some time.

I moved down a crowded avenue watching it slope and drop out of sight beyond my limits, as if swallowed by the curve of the earth. I smelled bread baking, the yeast making everyone on the street itch. My eyes got stuck to the ground ahead of me. Broken glass, strands of hair, a woman wearing a dozen pieces of patina jewelry yelling at a police officer. The sound of shoes on stone clogged my ears until the sharp bell of a shop door shattered my concentration. My eyes lifted and I realized just how many remnants of buildings were still lived in, scattered like a dark star exploded across the landscape.

Everything had a film of dirt, grimy with tobacco smoke, the machine's leaking oil. Deprivation and onionskin. I could feel the scrape of passing fingernails, could see the scabby dirt crammed underneath each one, even from across the street.

I drew near several vendors, each smelling like a dirty oven. I bought a dented money clip, at discount, from one of those suitcase women whom my mother used to invite into our home for lavender liqueur and biscuits. I had forgotten entirely that we lived on this side of town, just up the street, for a fragment of my childhood. No one tried to remember me, but everyone recognized my coin. I chose an empty money clip with the hope that I could continue to fill it, so that I might leave this city for good.

That was always the plan.

She threw in a tube of slightly used lipstick. The waxy coating made my lips look like rotting dahlia petals cut by the aging edge of my cupid's bow.

I felt fulfilled enough.

A boy was stuck to her skirts offering his own service. I paid him to draw me a scene of the city we were supposed to love. In response to my request, I received a heavy pattern of thick charcoal lines, which he folded over onto itself and rubbed out a mirror image on the opposite side of the sheet. He scattered long stars for street lamps and said to me: *Each line is a wall. Each star is a future.* When it was finished, I held a playground of directions, a key unlocking a tiny door in the mouth of an eagle.

Each time I shifted my right leg, my few remaining coins pulled at the cloth of my pocket, knocking the front crease coolly onto my crotch. I paid the boy double and continued on, swaying my leg to feel myself harden more and more.

My blood pumped as best it could to better move the cog at the center. I wrapped my arms round myself tighter for the walk back to the room I was happy again to share.

Why do they all call you Yin-Yang?
What do they call you on your island?

I rested my hand on M's knee, where the khaki was starting to thin on my uniform trousers. He had taken to wearing them frequently without asking, becoming more like me than I, myself, in a long time. He was losing his precious curves with every lost pound of fat and flesh.

I'm nobody. Only a project. Of your divinity. The work in progress. The silent poet. Will you stay with me tonight?

I twisted on the bench. We were lunching in M's favorite corner garden, now overrun with Heidelbeeren and rotten horse chestnuts. Twenty-minute stroll from home, but only five minutes from our latest clubhouse. I vacillate.

Your eyes may stand still, but they make me dance.
You dance for money.
I dance for no one. Or just a nobody. I laugh.
Why do they call you Yin-Yang? What shall I say?

I come from all sides. I circle round you. I am your prayer. Hunting. I am your mother. Feeding. Letting you feed. I balance between. I am something they cannot fully understand, for now they try.

I disrupted his smooth eyebrow with my cheek. I licked my thumb and pressed it to his chapped lips before he could pull away. He sat, stock still, staring between my eyes.

One light eye, one dark. My mother once said I could never trust you.

And this is why I'll leave you. Let's go home.
I'll only leave you if you make me change back to who we were.

His challenge roused me. I kissed the inside of his ear, where he had plucked the hairs away and raw freckles bled a new palette. He was wearing my favorite rouge on an otherwise blank face.

A new copper necklace knocked against his chest. I don't know where he got the thing, but it wasn't from me.

I was sweating beneath my wool coat, shirt sticking to the burn scars in full bloom in the autumn humidity. The berries were getting ready to drop and I could tell M wanted to pick and eat the sour buds.

I was colonized by the rows of his teeth that, I knew, would never stop ripping at me. He would get to grow old and I, I would stay sweat-stuck to a bench dedicated to war with a plaque so rusted it is unreadable and weeds latched on to each board.

When I finally got him home, I fucked him until he swore.

I started another war between walls made of paper and a trench carved out of sand.

Scheißen.

Our bodies devouring whatever potential the other held within.

Our slightest movement attacks his
metal throat splitting
cracking into the shell of earth
cut open oil slick
we're like you
iridescent on the
inside

Dried up wild
hop roots swerve
on razor blades
here

Snakes balled into knots
searching for thirst
underneath

A taste for blood
you climb bleached walls
a blank canvas
taking on the weight of
after

Everything else is about to happen
to you
now

What he might desire is as elusive as the reasons of a howling cat. All it seems to be is a want to be in the light. To be alight, as naked and blushing as he can possibly be. A waterfall of long lashes, he closed his eyes to change the perspective, moving the walls of delightful ruin. He became a woman many times before my eyes. How I loved her, to my own bosom and beyond. And then, as suddenly, he would change back in the middle of the night, until I could no longer tell the difference.

I am unsure how much longer my pension will carry us. I will have to take more jobs, johns and johns to keep the sweetness of this. A coin on the bed stand. Such a graceful thought, to love the dance. He is working as much as he can for now. He asks me, *Should I be working harder.*

What more should we want?

I have always known the aloneness of truth, always threatening to peel off my scarred skin, acknowledging the power, it might have if another wore it. No, he'll never be truly alone. So, he'll always sleep well. And I cannot surrender to that potential ruin. Robbing the night of its secrets. Pocketing someone else's murder weapon. What would his army say to such a poison? To ruin the largest figure of man we all know. What a glittering crusade that would be. The birds will not miss us when we're finally gone.

He cruelly thumbs my scars in the bathtub. Such wars, it seems, only he is obliged to ignore. A delicate partner must be somewhere, waiting to share this portion of the story. While posing strong, with shyness as a mask, he raises his eyelashes once again and gently flexes his nose, scanning the room already sinking in feathers.

Charcoal lines float beneath the surface of the bathwater, bending and growing between our legs, swimming in this oil tank. Every hour lost to staring at each other. My big toe pulls at his chest hair, grabbing at the fine stiffness of curved muscle and bones thicker than my own.

Margaret! Tonight, I say this foreign beast will be Margaret, fowl beast of the daylight and oceans far away. You, moesen saft! Look at me, Margaret. Show me your möpse.

Tanz. Tanz. Tanz.

I anchor myself with the ice of my drink and then spit it into his mouth, half melted – enough for him to crush the cube easily with his back teeth, as is his pleasure. We are, where exactly? A German club with a French name. Wearing mother's dresses that accentuate my straight hips, and my thick ankles on which the leather of my strappy heel peels against the sweat dripping from the creases behind my knees.

Margaret is crawling on the parquetry, pressing her tongue against everyone's ankles but mine. She seems to be avoiding me because I made her mouth so cold.

This whole game is foolish, I say.

I can see the bulge grow in her holey underwear quivering when she sits on her knees and pants like a thirsty pet. Klaus gives her bourbon ice, which she then drops between the breasts of our faithful Gem. Her slip reveals a wet trail down the front. I can see where the cube disintegrates in a glossy spot on the nest of her crotch. I don't believe she's wearing underwear.

Whenever she's around, I can't get a lick, let alone a smile. These sisters-at-arms circling around each other in the dust, scuffing up their elbows and knees. They're after new scars tonight. Such fun is meant for Thursday evenings. The mourning doves seem to multiply: caging themselves in the pile of our best winter coats, then emerging as two women, three women, a hundred times more women than ever before.

Their skins vibrate, barefoot and slipping around our bodies with the ease of hollow bones. The grace of a thousand falling feathers. I think about catching them in my hawk's mouth and breaking each skinny little thing, one at a time.

Moses. Sweet Moses, take me home. I'm tired and need your lips, the lips of an innocent commandant, to tuck me into bed.

The Gem sinks between Moses' legs and I can see him squeeze them together so tight he makes her body shake with his. And I miss my M. I desire his return to me. The two of them fall apart even further. This night has really cracked open. I pull his precious string of pearls from his coat pocket and drop them in my glass, hoping he will accept the insult as invitation and swallow me down too.

I want a new drink, one not so watery. The pearls root and blossom into lily of the valley at the bottom of my glass.

Attention, attention, one and all. This seal pup, stranded on the concrete sands of our humble city needs a name. Ideas! Ideas! Klaus's hand jumps to toast another christening and crashes into the chandelier, splitting light across our foreheads. The sound of breaking. He hides his head beneath the back of my skirts and stays there while half-decent proposals are made.

Minxsy. What about Minxsy? I've always loved a good minx.

Bourge, bourgeoi, bourgeoisie. Take your putzig ass home! Call him Maximilian and conquer me, me, me.

Call her Me-Me then and let's settle this. She'll be Me and I'll be Her and he'll be Simon. Simon says, smile.

Klaus's mouth moves from between my legs. His face pressed taught against my creamy slip. My turn: *Simon says, tanz.*

Tanz. Tanz. Tanz.

Dead flies dripping with honey
from the mouth between her legs
Suck on the lace wings

Spit the honey into her ear
Trace her horn

Eyes for days in tandem dance
Will serve as witness to

Slide onto her lap
Pucker up
Now chew

The morning is pastel and not a crisis in sight. M and I have started a new game in which we steal the happenings of the day and turn ourselves into breaking news.

We take stacks of newspapers off the stand, bring them home and quickly hide ourselves inside, cutting out the shapes of our hands on page eight and again on fourteen. We make vile shapes in the want ads and draw stars through the dullest headlines.

On M's supposed birthday, we leave greasy lipstick stains on page twenty-six. We wrinkle and fold page three so that the article carries a better bi-line, tells the story of how she was born. A story no one has heard before, but one she's told a million times before and many more since.

I swing M like an empty hammock between my legs and when my arms feel like they are going to quit he locks his thighs around my waist. I'm standing on the mattress. We've moved it to the floor. His womanhood is tied to the bed frame, sleeping off the long night. His legs are a horizon, parallel with the floor. Mine are spread equal distance, erect. Erect. I am his easel. He pulls at the scarves around my neck to put me off balance, but my bare toes cling to the mattress buttons. His shoulders quake, shaking out sweat. Tiny droplets, his juice patterns the cushion, making my toes slip together. I need to trim our toenails.

His heels click out a rhythm:

```
        ..-. / .. / -. / -.. -..-. -- / . -..-. .... / ..
/ -.. / . -..-. -- / . -..-. ..-. / .. / -. / -.. -..-.
-- / . -..-. .... / .. / -.. / . -..-. -- / .
```

I feel it through his leg muscles. His blonde hairs wrap around my curls.

I snatch for the grapes we stole from a street cart. They are dusty purple, wrinkled at the hole from which they were born. The stems, little bird's feet shriveled up and brittle, cover the floor.

Our romance might be turning stiff and stale like the grapevine in winter.

But it's hot now. How I love the summer. Another summer. The machine outside gets angry at its own steam and what's left of the royal family has taken to riding their white horses at dusk. How he loves their white horses.

I reach for more grapes.

I spit in his face. He taps out a rhythm:

```
    - / .- / -. / --.. -..-. - / .- / -. / --.. -..-
. - / .- / -. / --..
```

81

I drop him and his ass sticks in the air like a green pear resting in a cotton basket. His body is August tan and eyes still ice blue. His ass crack curves into a stem from which he is ripened and plucked.

Clap ha
take us home
silk screened darlings
and we take the nails from your bed

Slap ha
feel our bone threads
fraying under rooster claws
sharpened by hot streets and
sunrise stories

Clasp hands
find the song
Sing hands sing

Smack ha
twist our voice on
a record buzzing

Turn it up
turn up the sirens
save the story or lose us to
the stay away
future

Everyone is ha
having a brilliant time
inside your mouth

The cobblestones wobble under our feet as we make a grand gesture of waltzing through the square on a Sunday evening. Traffic has increased a thousand-fold since this square, in the shape of a teardrop, was opened to the public. It used to be where the royals would parade their finest garments and horses. These wide assed animals would bounce, sword on one side and pistol on the other. For a while, the horses were still shiny, unaware that they were splashing sewage water into the creases of their hindquarters. A rumor has spread that the horses were sold for meat to a hungry cousin and that's why the square became a public place for solicitation, taxi service, and on this day, our waltzing.

Happily, the fountain still flows, cold and golden. We approach the edge and test the temperature with brittle fingertips, then run our hands through each other's hair. Rounds of rust have stained the bottom where tossed coins once sprouted wistful dreams. M tiptoes around the edge to be sure the whole purse has been emptied, then turns toward me, closes his eyes and tosses a few münzen over his shoulder. I want to smash the fountain with the butt of a rifle. Let it wash this scene, expose ivory beneath all the blackened stone.

When the two officers appear, we are sitting on the edge, holding each other round the waist with legs French braided.

There's a lot of noise tonight. Plural sounds. My ears tremble. I can even hear the stretching of my ribs toward the hot purple sky. I close my eyes and imagine the horses parading by in full dressage just for us. We wish for new bodies in this concourse of noise. My eyes might be redder when I open them again. Our intoxication has caught the attention of the batonned men, now clopping toward us, *Guten abend meine damen.* The darkening sky now seems made of their rigid uniforms, so I point my chin upwards and swallow the strength to perform.

I lift M from his seat and turn him around, bucking his legs apart as if to frisk him on behalf of the authorities. Instead, I cock my arms above my head, hands pointing in the shape of guns, and begin thrusting quickly, my saggy crotch against his bony ass. My laugh bounces off the crooked buildings and chips away M's teeth, his smile a clownish grin reflected in the still water. Pleased at this puppet show, one officer takes his weapon and pats my ass with it, encouraging me to buck faster. The other one covers his hot face with both hands, and muffled, begs us to stop, *please stop*. In English. I don't stop until I feign satisfaction.

The pockmarks of the city's concrete seem like goose bumps on dry skin to me, in this moment. We shutter our bodies back into the street and bow, in tandem, for the officers who applaud with delight. The whole show free of charge and our nipples hard at the game of risk well played. I can see alkaline bubbles of rapid breath dripping from M's mouth. To finish I offer our audience a free ride and they happily banish our duo back to the slums. We leave the square to its noise, gently patting each other's backs and laughing at the lucky acceptance of our improvisation. They might yet kill us for that pleasure we hold so close. The city's mood is changing. The authorities are manufacturing morals again to beat back and bury citizen dreams. I am reminded that wars never travel far from us, their finest makers.

I light candles in every corner of the room, tall pillars that melt along the warp of the floor. We've lost electricity again. The full moon is faking heat, magnifying the silver in each flame. We have just beaten out the mattress and flopped it over the balcony railing so that it might air out what's left of our musty summer sweat. The smell of fur is heavy. I love beating the contents of this apartment, ridding crevices of the infectious scent of aging, squeezing old spider's eggs into grainy water. My cleaning bucket is so brown it reminds me of the basin filled with holy water at the church down the way. That water is made brown by all those dirty hands dipped in prayer. I bless the floor and the walls and the window; humming a hymn I cannot recall the words to. My shoulders ache. I attack an itch along my spine using puckered fingers and my shirt sticks to my skin.

We detach the webs from the dishes that are not cracked and lick the dust off my finest glassware, all chipped. Here and there, some old lipstick tattoos the rim. The candle flame flicks against my mother's lamp on the dresser, its cold green glass reflected onto the wall in the fashion of a prism. I feel as though a cigarette is burning holes in me, wishing that I hadn't agreed to host the party tonight.

M left to avoid cleaning duty. He patterned his speech to his heavy step down the stair: *Don't. Work. Too. Hard. Sir.* Called after me in off key song: *Pimpfish, pimpfish. Your pimpfish shall return.* That name I betrothed upon him. He left to find bread and hard cheese. At times I forget he is still with me. I am less and less able to retrieve my body from this dirty bucket, always searching for a blessing or two to call my own.

I have wiped the tin washbasin back to white, and emptied the glass ashtray, thick and marbled. I've dusted the lamp, the only source of unnatural light. It seems happy to do its job. The red shade winks back at me. I jump when passing the window, startled by the dead body slumped over the railing, then laugh at my own foolishness. The mattress is just another story in stains. It has been held between legs and covered in briny drool, but it is not dead yet.

I sink into the navy armchair, my favorite and only. Its cloth rubbed raw; some kind of crust runs down the side leading to the right armrest. I release a cloud, a glittering of dust and smells of wet paper. The chair has brass nails bolstered along the head and arms, once shiny now brown with age, dark wood legs cut into lion's paws. I can feel the springs hard in my ass.

I am proud of my linens. I wash them with military speed and the consciousness of a student holding her first bad grade. Woven crudely, stitches in tight loops of indigo. The crass thread feels like leg hair, and smells hoppy. The landlord provided them, along with the table, the chair, and the bed. In the beginning, he offered more assistance to us veterans. Now, he looks to the light bulbs when we pass on the stairs. This is not a punishment of me alone. He ignores the whole building, leaves nails poking up from the floor and laundry steam sweating the wood panels. There's a dark green mold where each wall meets the ground and the ceiling. *Opfer des krieges,* I hear him whispering again and again.

I am proud of my space, the single room without its own toilet and a small half wall with a cutout through which you can watch someone sleep and not be noticed. It separates the entryway from the bed, the closet, and my vanity. I can stick my hand through this window and wave goodbye to M. I can hang wet stockings to dry in this window.

The light comes down from outside in such a way that half my face is lit within the mirror, blinding one eye. I pay what is due for this room, on time, in cash. And I am thankful the men in charge of the slum prefer to leave us alone. There are too many tenants to count. Our bodies are stacked cans of food that simply won't perish, no matter how hard some may try.

I pull at spider webs, strung with sticky droplets of liquid, winding them tightly around my hand. There is one delicate spider at the north corner of the room. I leave her to her spinning. At one moment she is upside down, letting her legs stretch to the balcony. Staring back at me, she's wrapped a regretful fly and stashed it where she knows I can watch. She glides up to her tightly woven eggs. I dare not disturb this womb. I even have names for each of her brood, tiny things she may welcome while I'm still here. I list the names in pencil on the wall when I can't sleep.

M returns with bleach and a bouquet of lilacs ripped from the tree. One he insists is to help my ridiculous, obsessive scrubbing and the other is to feed my affections. Cheese was too expensive and he ate the bread on his way back, shared with a few boys in the neighborhood. His nose is red, and he takes off his socks and just leaves them, balled, on the floor. The lamp flickers in a code he seems to agree with. He moves to the three-legged stool in front of the mirror and watches me pick up his socks through the glass.

His delicate nature: a dab of warm spit on a piece of ripped cotton.

With two fingers he defrosts the makeup from my face. I am old bone, bleached in streaks from last night's ballroom. He knows not to ask where I ended up. More and more he stays behind, in bed, in dirty underwear. He makes sure all the white grease comes off before stripping me all the way down in the early sun. Cold metal light cuts through the shades, burning what's left of the chair.

He makes sure all the grease comes off with the acid of his spit, then he swallows my whole mouth, tastes himself, until I fall asleep.

We wake up in the dark and smother each other, falling back asleep only after our pajamas are left in a steaming pile on the floor. We light our cigarettes with filaments dipped in the accelerant of our sweat.

M is too quiet, silent animal, as if just given birth. His breath is always the same rhythm, barely a snore. Every morning we sleep late. His Adam's apple is like a fast-beating chickadee. I wake up to my thick hands glued to his thinning hair.

He takes off my eyelashes, says too loudly: *Don't disappear. I want to love you just as you are.*

He taps a warm, middle finger into the hollow behind my jaw.

       -. / . / ...- / . / .-. -..-. .-.. / . / .- / ...- / ...- / . -..-. -- / .

Two mourning doves balance on a thick, black railing at the top of the city, persistent sweets emerge from a silk bag nestled between them. They binge on these naughty seeds, giggling at each little burp, letting the powdered sugar fall into their feathers. They tip their heads around each other's faces, avoiding the sharp point of their red, little beaks. Butting foreheads occasionally, their conversation points into the shadows they cast down the spine of the city.

Below, the buildings are on fire. Clamoring bodies in the city's oven, the streets blackening hard and flaking under the hot breath of its citizens. Around each corner for miles, the same banner has been pasted to the sides of broken walls. Rumors of a new state cause fly on the breeze. The cheap paper sticks to passerby, it bubbles and roars. People are starting to listen to, to believe in, nonsense. The doves sigh, *Not again.*

The traffic sounds like a ring of keys swinging in the hand of a man walking with steady purpose. Sunday's laundry freezes and blows to the south on dirty lines sewn across courtyards that double as hop-scotch arenas and unemployment lines. The smell of cooking sausage makes its way through alleyways and into the caves where commuters buy their newspapers. Someone yells, *Verkauf.* Another voice sings, *Gott und Land.* Three windows break at the same time, for different reasons. A woman's black eye begins to heal.

The mourning doves are slender and tall with feathers of silver and pink. Their skirts molt a little with each rocking gesture, sending remnants of their wings aloft. Their tender claws grip to the railing as if in anticipation of a long nap. The song of the city soothes their hunger and their fear. *We will survive you,* they say. Their conversation caresses the nervous system of the land, humming a chorus from the wires alive with sparks of shoddy electricity. The doves survey their territory; this city cut out of compacted stone with a serrated blade. They stab long fingernails into one sour fruit candy after another. Watching and feasting. Feasting and watching.

We work hard for the stash
of stars
tucked in a cigarette box

Warp us with used cellophane
strangle us so we don't have to watch

Swallow the sweet vector's honey

Dance for us
we grind to the hum of high wires

We bully you boys into late nights
the dirtying of tongues

We milk the rigid bones of sleep
and then fresh daylight arrives

crusty with blood stains

It had been another late night. A slow ascending morning, and then the afternoon fell hard as if willing the evening's unfortunate events. I pretended to read some book M brought home from a curbside box. My scars were itching. It's how I know there's trouble coming. I was struggling to stay cool in the early heat of May. The cherry blossoms were returning to us, and the weeds were already springing from cracks in the rubble. This season, instead of reflecting pink on the fingerprint-smudged windows, the cherry petals are white like M's cuticles. Somehow, this makes them smell less sweet. The weeds, though, they always look the same.

I found the letters M did not want me to find, a correspondence that made me chew my nails until they threatened to bleed.

The author seemed to share his crises of time, the same paralysis, the same ruddy sensuality woven with a deep starvation that only permanent, inner war can sustain. The same privilege, but even worse. His hidden affair, this pen pal, gets more words than I ever do. No translation needed.

It was these letters that I actually read, tucked into the book. As the sun sank below the rooftop adjacent to our window, I grew weary of the hand written script and hungrier than I cared to admit.

I was hungry but not interested in food. The words tended to drift in circles around themselves, with no ending, no arrival or departure. Earlier, I had taken my mother's suitcase down from the closet shelf and put it under the bed, without blowing the dust off. M would never notice the old leather box, custom built for a retreat my mother missed. He had been out all day anyway.

When I arrived at the bar for a weak looking sandwich and a pint, I had missed the crucial blows, but there he was, the only witness on a quiet Tuesday. I could hear the *tap tap tap* of his metal heel from around the corner, claiming again and again:

- / --- / --- -..-. .-.. / .- / - / . -..-. - /
--- / --- -..-. .-.. / .- / - / .

The story goes like this: Two officers patrol our city block. They laugh dangerously, loudly with uncertain purpose, like we are the moral joke in a political comic strip. They are propaganda. They have raw scabs on their knuckles, are experts with a baton. They are brick-shaped men with an atmosphere of trick about them, and insecurity clouding youthful fantasies of a stairway to a golden eagle's nest, lined with fine art they'll never understand. They patrol the curb looking out for a smile or a cold face to slap, never for the opportunity to help an abandoned mother tapped dry of her breast milk or to save the child's stomach with a powdered sugar treat or piece of meat.

M flirts with the newsboys. He's more comfortable after these few years, more at ease showing a little leg. He whistles a greeting to the handsome blind woman begging beneath the budding trees across the street. The sunken sun has cast an indigo light through the slits of alleyways, wrapping everyone's skin in a strange rose color, plastering the buildings with a sense of sickly resignation. The weariness of stray garbage clogs the streets: a child's sock, broken bottles, soap bubbles running down from the butcher's shop, about to close. The dirt floats away with flaky shards of skin and chewy pig veins stuck in the rainbow of translucent suds, catching the last traces of light. It all washes eastward, through the tread of M's boot. He is rooted to the curb. He lets the boy suffocate. And I watch him, watching this sacrifice. I watch the corners of his mouth turn the wrong way. I mourn with the awareness that this is our final goodbye.

I turn my back to him and the doves stop singing.

Go to your tomb, we will bury you

in hot dirt   cauterize your memory
become us   and say goodnight

Tie your stories tight, to the hem

of your skirt   the skirt we granted you
wild tomb   go back to the sea

In a glass casket, pray for him

pray for all,   the we that is
a chorus line   form sea legs

Your caviar currency, couldn't work always

your salty tongue   debt of a slow dance
we won't show up   in the pictures

Of the night, we spent drowning in

your hands   pink blossoms to shake
your arms   white roots to choke

On the memory of

The story goes like this: The officers had been drinking since lunch hour. This was clear by their loud songs echoing off the building slabs and tearing on broken windows. They strode down the street, occasionally twisting their ankles in the cracks between cobblestones, leaning shoulder-to-shoulder, sanctioned hats in hand. When the kid ran out of the butcher shop, he tripped over their playful goose steps, as if these legs were cocked mousetraps and he the kid mouse blind and deaf with hunger. The ham hock sailed from his small grip and split apart at the feet of the butcher. The butcher was still scrubbing his stained curb and quickly realized the mouse had somehow stolen the carcass from the highest shelf.

The officers' song was cut short by the trilling avalanche of the boy's gypsy bells, loose round his neck, they made music with the curb as his skin scraped into the cascading soap bubbles. His body lifted itself onto his wet and naked elbows. His black eyes sank into fragile, brown skin smudged with dirt and his mother's homemade rouge. He stared up at the officers who hesitated for one brief moment, considering a hunter's choice.

Batons emerged in slow motion from the belted crotch of their uniforms and fell hard into the boy's crooked arms. Beneath his skin, bones splintered and cut into thin tissue. This tearing apart could not be heard from the outside, even the pain was a silent wonder. The boy's chapped lips opened in an O so big his ghost alighted on the breeze. Their untied boots disrobe him, beginning at his bellybutton. His clothing did not rip so much as disintegrate a little more with each impact. His cheeks are burned into craters with their lit cigars, the ash of which flew into the gristle of ham already headed to the garbage.

Doors shut wordlessly. In order to get home on time, the butcher sidestepped past the scene with his back flat against the brick. He was breathing through his nose and did not do anything to stop what was to come.

Hitting the bottom of a sinkhole, the boy lost sensation, could not feel his ankles pop. His scalp peeled back from his forehead. His black curls got stuck in the pores of the sidewalk. The mud of whatever lives between skin and skull mingled with lukewarm puddles of ammonia and the dirty suds. He became something crushed. Something drowned.

The small audience down the street had stopped talking, were watching in hesitant awe of the empty grip the boy still made with his fists and the only sound, those bells grinding out a final song between opened skin and concrete. The newsboys slunk back towards the boarding house. The blind woman palmed her ears. Only M stood straight, judging the scene. He did not try to stop this or move the body from where it was finally left alone.

A cat slipped by, en route to its nightly feeding, a saucer of milk and a cow's eye, left outside the butcher's backdoor.

I'll perform a disappearing act, I must. I will layer a million shreds of excuses on top of one another so as to feel brave and thick and warm. I am efficient in my suspicion of his dumb witness. Freedom, independence, self-sufficiency creating some hymnal resonance that he sends through the dead boy's body. No matter which season we are in, I am now cold.

What quiet, violent things escape our judgment with or without a true account? I heard the story. Saw the body and now I can't find M anywhere.

What self hangs here, at the end of a rope tied around his neck and falling to the mossy floor of the coastline forest M tells stories about, over and over again. I take great pleasure and then great fear from the weeds that root in the gaps of his easy mind. Now is my chance. I will have to kill him by turning him into a site of neglect.

I will pack up the stories he chose not to tell. I cannot forgive my own actions in the face of a rising night; how could he feast on such a scene. Feasting and watching.

I empty the closet; fold his secret letters into airplanes headed for the waste bin. Ignorant of all the facts, he showers me with fondness when he returns home. I'm afraid of what results from his gaze. I realize there is a disease beneath his bones, tumors that multiply. A contagion of voices. As he sleeps beside me, I can feel the infection getting closer.

It is high time to rip out the wart, roots and all.

Before he fell asleep, we held each other for the last time; then I wrapped him tight in the rotting seaweed of a bankrupt beach far away.

I'll never not follow you, I lie, forever weary of how the tides will work against us. Choking on the dead boy at the bottom of my throat, I drag myself out the door. My last look:

> M, trying to solder his heart back together with our familiar song. He is getting on board another ship, surviving the long journey home. He remains convinced I am still with him, that I will never not follow

him.

We will arrive in June, with the letters and remnants of the doves' song.

He wanders: a dreamer of choruses, a dreamer of our old mirrored bliss, until it breaks because I was never there at all. A dreamer he remains, because I no longer can be.

Come find Shangri-La
Heal your wounds, Stranger
        in the basement of beauty
Discount for a friend
        tonight only
First show on us
        second show on you

Return to Shangri-La
Heal your wounds, Sailor
        on a piece of floating stone
Discount for your many friends
        tonight only
Second show was for us
        third show is you

This is no longer my story. I want to make it harder on him: make his mind a complex system of trade winds and lover's beating veins. Break him when he realizes that our lust and attention was only a stubborn idea born from the sleep of his blue-blind eyes.

Restrain him and avoid the mess. This will all be gone soon.

Swallow us all. Choke on your own tongue, sweet M.

I consider stealing his story, somehow retreating without danger to stronger places, myself stronger, decorated in bestial pride.

The doves still sing our song, but we are both far away.

I consider stealing his collected objects, down to the post and frame. Ripping that calm smell from his seams.

Rust and oil and cut glass, melt it together and place a wick at the center. Burn it down.

Shave the skin off this place and wear the fur out of town.

I disguise myself so he'll never find me.

This place has become a stomach full of my relinquished pa-
tronage, I depart with starving eyes, a dry throat. Searching for a safe
place to rest. *Ta ta.* I will not fight another war. You cannot kill me.

A piece of M is still on that street, watching the weight of
this city's future drain from the boy's now grey body. When I think
about it, I pull the roots of my hair and scrub my skin to the color of
a wound. I have painted words in my own blood onto these buildings
and washed myself with these shattered shop windows.

Walking away now, flicking his pearls as they jostle in my
pocket. Who gets murdered and who gets the opulent choice of life?
Does he, alone, get to stand on the border of possibility while we fall
short of every unreasonable expectation?

I leave him naked in the bed, twitching his nails on the bedpost, what I know to be an account of his life:

    .. -..-. -.. / .. / -.. -..-. -. / --- / - /
.... / .. / -. / --.

And again:

    .. -..-. -.. / .. / -.. -..-. -. / --- / - /
.... / .. / -. / --.

And again:

    .. -..-. -.. / .. / -.. -..-. -. / --- / - /
.... / .. / -. / --. -..-. .-- / .-. / --- / -. / --.

I elevated this man, wrapped him in my velvety web, filled him with my eggs, made a proud woman of him and still he sunk into the muddy foundation of what must always be built and rebuilt. Full steam ahead, again and again. I want no part.

I do not think I have packed as much confidence as I will need. I have known all the alleys. I scraped his back against tree bark and used both hands to torture him. *Get down. Close your eyes. Open your mouth.* I, too, have burned my knees on hot tar. I've loved the melting bed of thirsty, dreamy bodies. I have been spread across an entire afternoon, drunk with the mourning doves in this abandoned paradise. Blinded by the sheer scarves of our imagined memories. I swallowed my own vomit when I let him live inside me. I've survived the quiet hour when I walked away alone; afraid I will not make it to my next bed. I have burned with guilt and trembled in the small space of relief when I got away with a bad thing.

I taste future secrets in the last sip of wine from his glass. I tell myself; I needed this one, those thighs around my waist. He wanted the seed, so I am embedded in him. I will reemerge after this very long day in the sun, having created a burr he can't shake loose. He'll take me back to where no one knows all that he's accomplished. Inside him, I will pressurize our story into metal plates of a shared legacy. I'll monopolize his attention behind closed doors. I don't care for his feelings anymore. I'll create a more human scene, his flesh slick with the oil of hurt but left breathing. I will pour whispers into his ear again and again.

Unwrap the quiet ones
who all think their first ride is so special

Spin faster spin faster exhaust and spin
Mother of pearl mirrors and camouflage face paint

What circus here released that buzzing of flies
brighter than in the spring weeds of away away

Oh voluptuous tensions
Oh the sweat sliding along his rib cage

Of lobster festivals and lady slipper parades
Remember our thawing winter in the gutters of Berlin

The mattress holds his wrists and our hips
pinned to each other's leather

Someone close apologizes the power to breathe gold
inflating the night with cheap whiskey and feathers

Oh the richness of pageantry
Oh the blood of an unhealed wound

With teeth of perfection a nobody can call us darlings
In a whisp of hunger we come home again and lose again

Into the velvety gills of him
an unwrapping of the quiet ones

A traveler in love with the serenity of our white horse pose
We lick the creamiest of bones lying beneath furs

Oh a tongue kiss for the poor old gal
Oh the ecstatically disturbed, sun burning our soft tissues

BOOK III.

DOGTOWN

UNWRAPPING THE QUIET ONES

M's body disembarked the five o'clock ferry. The dock rocking with a slow breeze, easing him onto the dirt road, his movements are laborious as if he is on new legs once again. This time, bowed at the knees. It feels as much like solace as he could hope for. He had wanted to return a hero in the next story, but his eyes are darkened from road dreams. All he can taste, as the ferry exhausts itself out of reach, is that same old invisibility and a common insanity that suits his present mood all too well. He will regain some strength; begin hanging his body like the fishermen again, encode himself back into this landscape; tie back on the broken up boots his father died in.

He buys stale cigarettes off a woman who does not recognize him, but says to him anyway: *We're happy you're heah*, then *yes sah* and *ok*. The woman is caked with wrinkles. Her stance suggests that she hides something between her legs. From what M cares to remember, she was a wife of one of the drug hungry window men of his youth. Yes, Sally.

Sally. She looked better now, despite time passing, and she took him in. Lying with her like dirty spoons, he sleeps in her real goose down bed, in front of a small wood stove. The feather spines stick in him as he turns toward the wall over and over again. His skin gets so hot; he has to hang his limbs out from beneath her cover.

Her breasts dip inward at the top as if they've been pet too much and they drape almost to the middle of her rib cage, which moguls her thin skin. She eats saltines with butter thickly spread and drinks the cheapest vodka with orange juice.

She has short, fading hair. Thick eyelashes and always the strap of her slip sliding down the slope of her left shoulder blade. She likes the nape of her hair pulled after they toss the mattress. She has far spreading skin that wraps M in the temperature of the Atlantic on the first hot nights of June. Only used skin can do that.

This was all before the fun park opened, before the season got under way. M is a part of the empty background, still sometimes waking up in the soldier's bed, alone. Still stunned. The sun is getting stronger, but he's lost in the dark.

Sally is a storyteller and sings the same song every evening around a fire pit made of mica and granite. She calls him by his full name and makes him jewelry with shards of blue sea glass and fishing wire. She suggests he build a home here, perhaps the abandoned cottage off Church Road, half mile before you can make out the pirate ship at the park, now sinking off the dock. She does not remember that this was his father's house, where his mother left him, where he is afraid he'll hear old voices fly through the broken windows. All the tarnished chapters that came before will swaddle M in silence. He wants to fight against the hold but has forgotten how.

Sally enjoys his secrets as long as they're left unsaid. She pushes him through his night sweats, and then demands he wash her sheets. M enjoys being punished. She wants him to love her, but she is too salty. He craves the murky water of the cove, wants to chain a piece of slate to his ankle, and sink to the bottom. Yet, he soon dreams of the desert, sleep walking to another death. He can't hold still in this frozen frame. There's too much in the way, but they move in to the house anyway. In the mornings, he soaks up the puddles of fuel leaching from the ground beneath his father's shed and burns their breakfast.

There's an urge in his palms too great to resist. He rubs his eyes with it, creates new wounds. The pressure on his heart is a large boot pushing, dripping bloody, soapy mud into his arteries.

Dear M,

You've returned and I can see fissures in your skin. You've returned, for what? To bury sharp metal deep inside yourself. To hide again after such a strenuous journey and listless abandon. I can see the way an experience has ripped you open. Your return is timely, so much has changed. But what can you save? You've returned in order to escape again. From bearing witness to the death of more children in which you see yourself.

You will imagine boys with the full body of your man. Remember: he left you. Some of these boys will survive and lay beside you. Some of these boys will leave you again and again, as he did. Their voices will echo through each crevice you step over, each wave that breaks across your ankles. I will make sure your dreams are not made of peaceful song.

I am writing to you now, to work this out once and for all. What shows on my skin, I put on yours too. I'm making words in the form of chunks of muscle. Gristle and ass pimples and hangnails shape the words I have to get out. Onto you. There is much to say and I fear I am losing your attention, like you've forgotten I'm here too. But I am here and I'm not going anywhere.

Out of the corner of my eye, in the early morning, I too see the shadows that haunt you. I have decided they will haunt me too.

Yours truly,

THE SAILORS

Every night Sally's stories drive M into the damp air, to the pier, his feet alive only in the phosphorescence that the soldier dreamed of eating with both hands.

The longer he shares a pillow with her, the louder M is able to speak. He lets her stay, making soap, selling her jewelry and fortune stories to the high tide crowds that flock to the Tycoon's waning amusements. The price of admission has gone up, though the whole scene is a punch line now.

She says that he doesn't deserve her. She threatens to ruin his face, insists on meeting the men he talks to, and wants to know where we are hiding. M ignores her threats. And we, the Sailors, stay tucked behind M's ear. M doesn't really care for her. The addict despises the drug. He pushes her out of the bed and fondles himself in the sheets, then writes his notes on little slips of toilet paper:

.. -..-. -.. / .. / -.. -...-. -. / --- /
- / .... / .. / -. / --.

And:

.. -..-. - / .- / ... / - / . -...-. -.--
/ --- / ..- / .-. -...-. -... / .-.. / --- /
--- / -.. -..-. .. / -. -...-. -- / .. / -. /.

Only we understand. We, the Sailors, arrived on late June's tide. M manifested our uniforms and masochism, of course. He wants us to pin him down and gut him from hole to hole. We make happy the memory of what happened before. We skew it in his favor. Our rowdy choruses let him play out his own script. This is all just like last time, before he left, but louder and we are older right along with him.

It is a bit colder than other summers. We sleep well tucked safely within his folds, but we dream better with her bony ass dug into his stomach.

Before we haul him up every evening, he wraps her in copper wire until she glows as conductor, as a circuit for herself. He places her on the overgrown lawn; in case he returns home with some other new someone. M, always hedging his bets. She sleeps restlessly in her own glow as storm after storm rolls in.

Sally will disappear too, eventually. She can't stay in the midst of all our voices. She will creep her skinny ass back across the island with all the money she saved.

He explores the tide with us, the Sailors, and paints our faces to look like that lame soldier. He doesn't say much. We accept that he is without words, that he is not yet convinced we are real, which is fine. We already know his stories from beginning to beginning again.

We say to him, trying to make sense: That Sally, speaks in rhythms, codes that we do not understand. She cannot be as old as she looks in the morning. Age has nothing to do with it really, we're just trying to understand what makes her rule a room with such capital, and yet we remain invisible, behind all the newspapers she's insisted on pasting over each window. We admire her and so, torture her with M's body. We encourage them to each become the other.

M says, *I'm not good at being alone but I hate that you're here.*

Every Sunday, we throw M a party of one, kneeling in prayer on the beach, watching the first of the summer meteor showers rip through the velvet, navy sky. We drink her orange juice and teach M a few melancholy songs while kissing his toes with the surf.

He wants to leave Sally wrapped in her metal, mosaiced with her own sea glass, and thirsty. He explains to us: *I only write love letters to one woman and only she can answer me.*

Yes, M, we already know from where.

He has woken up in this place that he keeps trying not to love, and has found it changed. This place dies again and again. It has become the kind of rotten carcass that still grows scabs of long fur. He believes we understand this kind of death with guilty precision. Really, we just understand how to kill his memory and make something new. He skips stones into the raked-up sea. He sits by our side, silent, and we know.

He came back to the island to collect objective thoughts.

ORIGIN

M's feet come alive in the phosphorescence brought on by an excess of algae plumage. The colors of peacock feathers slip between his toes and make his ankles feel warmer than they should in the crisp Atlantic. Sally's stories sent him out into the night again and he fears running into his mother's skirts, but not enough to avoid eventually heading back to the bed she stained, to not do that would be unforgivable. He left Sally tied to that bed, wearing a faded nightgown that belonged to the mother. He sits alone now, without even his sailors to protect him. When next he looks down at his feet, his mother's are also there, dangling close by.

M: Tell me my birth story.

Mother: You were torn from me. [Rips at the wet air with her fingers shaped in hooks. He sees red dirt beneath her fingernails] My armpit was cut open and from the wound your feet sprung out. Your toes were long and the blood that we made smelled of dirty ice and rye seed.

M: Tell me how you healed.

Mother: I wrapped the wound in sheets of kelp. Told your father I would not return home until I could tell the story without closing my eyes. [Closes her eyes]

M: And I was with you?

Mother: You were with me.

M: I wasn't sure I belonged to you. Everyone sees my father on me, expecting me to dig holes the way he did, expecting me to look for some secret treasure in the sand. [Bores his index finger in a rotten knot of the dock, takes it out and flicks a stack of fish scales over his left shoulder]

Mother: He tells the story all wrong, but that's his long game. My stories are truth and carry with them the weight of the bodies that forgot to write themselves an ending.

M: When you disappeared, I wanted to go with you. He told me the Captain's story and I stayed even though I was not tricked. Then he died and I left, like you always feared I would. I never liked the winter here, just like you. [Shivers in spite of dawn approaching]

Mother: Your father would have you believe that the Captain coaxed him here and then his own hand dragged me, but that is not the way it is. I was called here just the same, but not by a monster. We each had our reasons for running away from our people's homes.

M: Tell me your story and I'll believe it all the way.

Mother: This place was a promise sent on ocean spray. My sisters had all left home for their own monsters. The promises these men told were spun in cheap fabric and I hated the smell of them. My mother begged me stay where I was, but then came a promise too great to resist.

M: A secret, I hope. [He smiles like he once did with the mourning doves]

Mother: Something I'll keep for myself because it didn't work out as I planned. This island was supposed to leave me be: alone and satisfied. This island ground me down to pulp and the men here stirred me in with their spit and their shit. Then you came and the space from which you grew ripped me open all the way from here to the tidal line. [Pointing to her pubic bone] You were born with teeth and red eyes, but only to me. My mother would not get out of my dreams and she warned me again and again, I had failed. I had failed and it was time to leave again. Do you remember the figure eights we used to draw in the sand?

M: I used to think that was my name.

Mother: And the people who would follow us on our walks, asking for favors and ushering ships to our feet?

M: They abandoned me when you disappeared, but now I believe they've come back to play. We don't really need you or your stories anymore. [Looks into that hollow knot in the dock and sees inside the many mouths of the sailors waiting for him around the bend in the road]

Mother: I often forgot about you. I would stand outside in the afternoon quiet, my arms out, the milk leaking out of my breasts. It wasn't until I had soaked through my dress that I ever even heard you crying.

M: You infected me with your dreams. What you thought was one way, became another wind. Your body formed the number three and then took his number three and you pushed the two threes together to make me. I am the figure of an eight, fused together by the thickness of your hair and his silent brutality.

Mother: You can see for yourself. Go see the stains still there on the chest of each dress I left for you.

M: What made you never love me?

Mother: The fear that you would surpass me some day and not need to stay here and then leave on a better boat. That you would become a woman of great strength. That you would take your life, so meaningful but useless, and tap out a new story full of lazy eyes and beautiful legs and hot bullets, fast trains, and many many hipbones. All of that spread thickly across the belly of a whale that you would devour single handedly.

M: [Grinds his ass into the wood, making his bones hurt. She has not moved since she showed up. She has not made any attempt to touch him like she used to] But I have no money anymore and no desire to remember all that I've seen.

Mother: I keep your memories sewed into the lining of a rib cage made of spruce, wrapped with heron's wing and secured to the bottom of this damn island so hard that not even your teeth could pull them free.

M: I've heard this story before.

Mother: I got your letter sealed with the Captain's spit. I've sent so many responses. Have you read them? I imagined each return postcard, addressed to the only thing I ever loved, signed: G R A C E. But you shouldn't believe anything I tell you. [Shivers and yanks at her breast. A dead moth falls out of her folds and sinks into the depths]

The volume of her voice has grown increasingly loud and M suddenly realizes that he doesn't miss her at all, but longs for his sailors deep in his gut. He wants their thick thighs, sealed in white uniform, to light his way back to the cottage. A black storm appears in the distance, beyond the horizon of pine trees on the next island over. This time, he leaves and she remains.

STRAIGHTENING CIRCUMSTANCE

By the middle of July, as more visitors drag their fine silk scarves and suitcases through grooves of the packed dirt road, a new twilight crowd gathers along the fence of the graveyard, at the far end of Church Road. Walking back with melting ice cream cones from the north point market, a young family might witness acts of intimacy in which fleshy, red parts of bodies touch other fleshy, red parts. The colors around these bodies change with shades of shrubbery and skin. This, of course, is not how it used to be, but M is thankful for a certain amount of freedom, however hard it may be for him to express it. He is thankful just to know that a change has blown in.

Even a woman can find some head if she sticks around long enough, pressed hard against a tree while rubbing someone else. M used to blush at the thought of it. Now, the air seems thick with all the border crossing one could hope for. His eyes water now at the thought, a smudge of mascara left over from his last, long journey rubs into the fat pads beneath his eyes. Someone attempts to wipe his face clean. Is he sweating? Nervous?

No, no, just a tear or two.

Boredom. Pleasure.

Discontent. Satisfaction.

Protest.

A desire to capitalize on desire.

Someone gets angry at the confident thrusting, *can't take one more second of this bullshit,* and the stickiness of the scene. What few police are left on the island tear through each body, their values tight around their belts.

A man in the nude was beaten last week until his blood kicked the grass. His thighs were dented in blue.

While hiding in the woods, M is forced to remember.

The old fishermen still sit round a table at the bar playing seven-card stud with quarters. And they still know how to tell a good ghost story and spit at his feet as he reinstates his night walking. They have never forgiven his father's death. They know how to hold a grudge, because some God or other gave up on them years ago. They've been taught to rely only on themselves for all the blessings and judgments of many lifetimes.

Shoulder to shoulder to forehead and heart.

The quiet life.

A blind circus.

A piece of dying sound.

Milk and eggs are expensive out here. The young woman at the grocery gently attaches orange stickers to each soggy carton, and says, *Gawn up every damn day.* She is dating one of the Ferris wheel operators. They grind in the freight shed, while the other kids play a clothing-swap game. Each pair of eyes gets a sneak peek at cute little titties and still soft pubic hair. The boys strap on their bras and denim skirts, fondle themselves for practice. They all stay out late singing choruses in the face of invisible curfews. Falling asleep in damp tents crawling, inside and out, with earwigs.

This is a game M knows how to play better, though he does not get involved.

The quiet ones don't say much of anything; they work their bodies so hard. Despite this, pretty soon they will not be able to afford their meat.

Dear M,

I mistook you for the small boy I once knew, patiently waiting for a spoonful of flesh.

Now, where has your appetite gone?

Swallowed, no doubt, by all these companions standing in the circle of our making. These aging companions smell delicious. They steal our breath; such pleasure you think you need to deny. You can't blame your head for trying to write the same story again and again.

Their voices fill the space; stealing the names we once called each other. With or without me, I like watching you fall in love. Be sure to take your medicine. You need a good night's sleep.

Yours truly,

MATINEE IDOL

We came to M on the pier. We were in full uniform, clean and respectable, but he wanted to assume we were dangerous on our best days. We followed him into a late-night film and later tied him up with a shredded tablecloth his woman was planning to use as rags. We made him count to one hundred before taking off the blindfold, then let him touch us with the delicacy of his puckered feet.

He refuses to leave the back porch, just sits and stares at the ditches between dunes. He says, *we should get a dog to feel safe and less lonely.* We say, you're not lonely, honey. You're tired, but all your parts still work.

He wants to eat our ears and then our lips to quiet what only he can hear.

We wear a necklace that he never takes off. Oxidized copper, a molded seal of a horse in mid stride. M doesn't mind until it breaks his front tooth, when he leans over the hammock, to kiss the air. He says his head hurts every time our lips meet. At a distance, a different part of him watches the sun disappear between our chapped and tender muscles.

We promised the soldier; we will not let him forget.

He wants to tell us a story we already know, of what happened before we came to be. Something of the places he's been. Dizzy arms. Sharp tongues. Grottos and basement parties dipped in melting gold. We have our own versions of his war. We share a cigarette with him, but we don't inhale.

We might follow him forever with loud, little reminders. One evening, he asks:

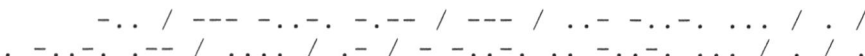

This time, no one answers.

FLICKER FANCY

M and his sailors take the three sharp turns down Church Road and maneuver their wide hips into the crusty seats of the modest, twenty-four hour film house, now showing filthy movies for free between midnight and two in the morning. His dates pick the best vantage point and then he falls into the chair closest to the aisle even though it creaks and wobbles left to right when he fidgets and he can't stop fidgeting. There are only a few others in the house, people M does not recognize even if they seem to take note of his father's face. No one seems bothered by the sailors, these hopeless tourists. They pose no threat to anyone other than M. Once settled, everyone stares forward with their bottom lips sticking out and their hands in their laps. Only slightly louder than M's odd whispers into the empty seats beside him, a conversation of objects begins on the brightening screen.

[If you watch closely you can see the sweat bubble up between leg hairs. The women do not shave their armpits in this one and that is just my favorite part. It makes me recall a place. Takes me away. This place smelled of tobacco and washed hair, sometimes cornstarch and blood. I formed new organs while walking its side streets. I became something beautiful and then I left the beauty behind]

A Mirror: Stares back into the eyes of a tired man as he flicks on a bedside lamp. The reflection flickers, revealing a naked body, dimpled in places. The cleft of his ass crack pure wanton, an empty vessel. Charcoal hairs sketched on his white chest, a mustache of the same color. Wet lips shine back into the man's face. He lies, prone and opens his legs. His image sighs and from behind him another body raises from the bed half draped in smooth, musty looking fabric. His reflection is all power and glow.

A Water Glass: Sits on the bedside table, half obscured by the man's body. Warped in the skinny curve of the highball, an equally skinny ass, a woman's, spreading a little bit as she raises herself on top of the man. Looking close enough, one can see hair sprouting there. [See, the hair is the best part] Sliding down, she opens, guides the man inside with her left hand. The water glass rocks, slightly, warping her image even more. They combine bodies along the lip of the glass, where water gently trembles but does not spill.

The Bedside Table: Is painted red with pale blue knobs whose facets mimic a cut diamond, matching the necklace stuck snugly between her swollen breasts, the only thing she wears, save for false eyelashes. [To have those breasts, and feel the weight of those stones. My god, grant me delight]

Those Pale Blue Knobs: Reflect the bodies one hundred different ways in each cloudy facet. The bodies shake, stacked on one another making the tiny, tiny reflections shake, making it look as though the bedside table is also shaking.

The Bedside Table: Gets knocked over as another man stumbles in from behind the mirror. This man is toweled by a piece of white linen, frayed at the edge. [Low budget is just the best, wouldn't you agree] This man is even more pale, a body M relates to his own and is therefore not as interested in. But his cock pulls at the towel and this is what the story is all about. [Where intimate rooms are filled and ruined]

The Water Glass: Falls against the table as this man cozies himself up to the other bodies, still fucking. Water spills across the thirsty wood. The same sound, water smacking wood, comes from the bed now, as things begin to boil over. The second man is still looking for a point of entry. Water everywhere. The light changes, suggesting other people off camera making decisions, allowing the water glass to move with the bodies then roll right out of sight.

The Light: Turns the color of limes then red, the color of their widened flesh.

The Mirror: Also rocks up and down with the movement on the bed. The second man has positioned the coupled bodies on their left side, granting him access to an ass. [See he already has nail marks down his back. They've done this scene over and over again]

A Sheet: Is smeared with the lightest pink when the first man peels himself away from the woman and wipes his cock on the mattress. He crinkles the sheet to form a nest and catches his breath with his eyes closed. He takes the sheet into his open smile just a bit, bites down. [Sustenance]

The Mattress: Is wiped with brown, viscous smear when the second man pushes the first away and lets his cock rest. He closes his right hand on the high cheekbone of the glittering woman. She appears to be falling asleep. The first man wraps his left hand around her throat. She smiles. [To be her. To be only her]

The Floor: Is wet and creaks with the weight of the bed and the weight of the bodies as they rearrange themselves to resume the waltz, displaying their facets of satisfaction in the mirror and the knobs and warped around the lenses of a pair of bifocals belonging to a director who cannot be seen. There is always a director, maneuvering each object, putting him and her at the proper angle. The floor buckles and smiles with the weight of this story.

[I'm partial to this one. Not so special, it just cuts to the quick of all we ever want and all we ever do to each other. Fuck, right? Fuck. Tiny wars. Love is making believe]

M and his sailors watch until the brief credits skew the line of sight to the bodies still tangled and humping. This creates a strange layering of perspective; blurring the bodies and making the words mean more than the action. Some patrons get up slowly and leave. Some clap. Others keep their hands in their laps. M stays until the last of the words fade from the screen then he takes his new companions back to the cottage. The projector stutters and closes its eye. Bodies still tangled, still humping.

Dear M,

You're placing your head on a chopping block and you'll lose your tongue before too long. Now, summer is leaving you too. I presume you'll run away again, drive yourself to another end. Set yourself on fire or at least rip the clothes from your body and let your body burn at the hands of a sun that will never make it as far north as you have lived.

I've got other places to go too, you know. Other people to play with, a legacy of tongues. Can't expect me to stay in the background while you fumble your way through scene after scene. It is my opinion this little exploration has circled back on itself and my work is almost done. You and I have gone just far enough.

We've invented something here, you and I. A list of characters with holes for eyes and someone else's life at their heels. I'll turn your disappearance into one more of these people. I'll dress him up in the stories not written here and bind him in the next chapter. And perhaps he'll give me what I need.

Yours truly,

DARK LANDSCAPES

M is remembering something that didn't happen in Dogtown. The memory started with a noise that trembled hard, up from the ground, through his heels, reaching for all the scabs picked raw at his center. It started with pressure in his ears and settled into a sideways glance toward what did happen here and everywhere else in between. He raises one eyebrow at the sight of us reflected in the mirror, unsure of how to translate this feeling. It's hot tonight, but he's the only one sweating, like trying to talk through the glass. He is wishing for the soldier to be here, instead. Wishing for him to be here now and not nowhere.

M leaves Dogtown in a dream, lets his mind travel on a rust flavored train to a place that stinks rotten. Piss and cocaine. Sure, it is much more exciting but tiring too. Tides go in reverse and he reminisces the way dirt once stained his bare feet. He thinks about the people he's loved, but everyone is in the wrong uniforms, resurrected saints who share his fascination for close up photographs and the flavor of black paper cigarettes. Spice. His returns to the city. He forgets the ocean is near.

When we leave him for good, some stains will remain. His hands blue, aging. Body vibrating high. The backside of his teeth taste like ground coffee beans, lips soft as frothy milk. Thoughts of more lovers, sleeping through future memory, in places now sunk or cut up by grains of sand.

Jealousy is easy. We could warn him that lonely months will follow. We could tell him his story will be under constant threat. But he'd rather get lost in our mops of hair and spit that turns bitter on the back of his throat. He uses Sally's lavender oil to sooth the rashes in his mind. Oh, he'll find something, someone. A salve. M has to get that good tingle along the collarbones, or else he'll drown. For now, we mix our liquid bodies with crushed mica and cattail spines and rub it across his chest.

THOSE AMOROUS BLUE EYES

A weak sun drips into M's bedroom window. He's taken the newspaper down. He raises his head to the top of his pillow. Twists and tweaks his nipples between thumb and forefinger until everyone is awake enough to make a fresh pot. Just for his sailors. He doesn't drink coffee anymore. Sally is long gone.

In his most persistent dream, saltwater barnacles get stuck under his eyelids. He cries briny blood until the creatures slide out the corners and he can see again. The pain does not frighten him, it's that his eyes turn to a rotten purple, the color of animal blood at dusk. He must remember that blood never looks purple. Purple is something at the end of a happy day. Blood drips black or blue from real wounds, real wounds that don't heal. He watches his blood sink into the ocean. That's how he knows he's dreaming. We, Sailors, read all this in the way he stares to the corner of the room and does not respond to our catcalls.

Every morning, the radio cracks the silence, playing the same set of music from a tower at the other end of the island. M presses his hand to the table:

        -.-. / --- / -- / . -..-. -.. / .- / -. / -.-. / .

        -.. / .- / -. / -.-. / . -..-. -.. / .- / -. /
-.-. / . -..-. -.. / .- / -. / -.-. / .

We skip a buttonhole on our freshly bleached shirt. We get dizzy with stars every time we stay over.

He makes soft-boiled eggs and hot buttered toast. A phone rings far off, and often, but he never answers. He tells us, *I prefer letters.* And he flicks his necklace hard onto our stone collarbone.

Dear M,

I imagine that you probably dream yourself into the body of that boy and watch your own skin beaten open. There are so many beatings, so many more to come, but really it's all the same.

Let's document what I imagine you dream about. I'll imprint the time you've spent and the time you cannot get away from. If all this looks similar to you, it's because we've been here before. Though the way the island survives has changed just as your body tells a different story. A witness to these events might wonder why you matter at all. Who is the story for exactly? An island in rot or a man on the run or a woman who has no more cause to sign her own name. My goals were maybe too selfish and now I can't stop using you. Using you to trap an audience the way you chain others to a bed or steal a coin purse or seal an unfortunate fate. All that's getting too heavy now and here you stand, ready to play again. How does boyhood taste now, now that you're on the other side?

I write through you to understand my memories and the patch work of past that represents our origin. Can't I own one thing? Can't it be you and your unfortunate actions, your avoidances? Silences and caresses. No one else will want you anyway.

A question asked many times before: has no story ever felt so crucial and yet so unimportant? For this I feel guilty and might kill you off just yet.

Yours truly,

DOGTOWN

Laundry is done on Sunday afternoons on the island. With the delicate, one eye-closed attention of a bloody hangover. Everyone stands out at the wash lines, blowing the sand off clothespins before fastening each sheet, every greasy pillowcase to the rope. Saturday nights demand a good washing of all these things. The sound of memoriam flags wave in and out of the hard winds. Their embroidered hems kiss the sandy grass plots down every block that skirts the water.

The beaches are empty until the washing is set out to dry. By two thirty, the fractal shadow of the Ferris wheel spins down onto the silhouette of M behind a king-sized sheet. Time to languish in the forgotten memories of every last night. The husky laughter of sailors, voices clogged with the good bits of all that's happened.

There is always a breeze on the island. It keeps the characters swirling in its ring and unable to leave. This place is called Dogtown because we're all phantoms here, lost artifacts of stories and fragments of truth, shattered by the harshness of a hungry animal, and then worn weary by the waves of this deserted haven.

Dogtown is knowing all the pragmatic ways of loving and then ignoring those who fall.

The townies spit into their warm beer cans.

Each stack of napkins on each picnic table in the shabby fun park is held down with a painted beach rock. Every wooden surface is soaked with puddles of old ice cream, oily crumbs, and body fluids.

The general store hasn't moved the pin up calendar from fifteen years ago. The cereal is all expired.

Dogtown solace is a sandblasted postcard.

A fossil.

Loneliness makes its own gravestone in Dogtown.

Everyone burns their skin.

Everyone falls in love.

PORTRAIT OF THOSE PALE EYES

We, Sailors, have the palest brown eyes, almost yellow. Skin the color of stained birch wood. We never apologize. It takes a long time to get us through a doorway. Our stare makes M hold on to the carousel too tight. We are never ready to leave the dark theater and we hold M there too. We orient M at the center of everything else that fills a room. We pierce the sour smells of dirty mouths smacking on olives through our eardrums. We drip brine into M's mouth, attacking his tongue with the used toothpicks. We languish in the rustle of M's leg hair. We crack a beer open with our right hand, but write secret notes on the mirror, in cursive, with our left.

We wear red and blue pocket squares in every shirt, every day. We refuse to be blindfolded during our long naps. We perform all these acts for M, alone. For us, the morning sun is always too bright. Like M, we prefer a sunset, when he can disappear into the dunes. Like M, we smell of homemade soap and diesel.

On that pier, we were covered in starched white, the color of a skeleton picked clean. Our hands were winter dry, but with fingernails finely manicured as if we'd been on leave for quite some time.

We tend to M obsessively, letting him sit like a common law king in a borrowed Adirondack chair, facing west in the morning and east in the evening.

In his more fanciful moments, M considers getting a uniform too. We all practice marching around the sandy yard. We teach him to murder the hanging sheets with a bayonet he found while hiding out in the attic of some dull party, a few weeks back. In these moments, we laugh and laugh.

One of us tells M:
We knew you were coming back long before you woke, alone in that other city.

Another searches:
If we thank you for taking us in would it be easier to relive your stories?

Another tells the truth:
We are happy to have you but we cannot save you. Now, you must go.

Dear M,

I wish I could be with you every morning to watch you eat, but I want to forget you by the night. Were I were there with you to watch each body reduced to geometry. Were I were there to listen to you explain yourself in the rhythms that I taught you. Your silent language is used to hurt things.

Is this what we intended by putting words to page?

I get the sense that your feelings are a sensitive color, the living muscle inside a shell. I can't help you in there, but I can squeeze a rind and make a wine that helps us both remember where we came from. That's what this is, isn't it?

There's a lot of blank space here I cannot account for. There's space where the paper betrays. A dead dog is buried beneath where you sit reading this. Only a memorial ahead of you, built with bad nails, and the shadow of it forms a whole new landscape.

Yours truly,

COLLECTING OBJECTS

Proteins and peptides abound. The still-young boys congregate around steamy noontide pools, mouthing each other and sharing their flavorless gum. They remain until their creamy spit sinks into the algae. Sterile now. Crab food and snail slime. They return to delaying foot traffic with their hockey goals made out of driftwood. Arcade after lunch.

A cloudy chandelier has been installed above the magic mirrors in the fun house. Très moderne. Girls in high-waisted bathing suits bend their knees in front of the melting glass. A nipple slips. The daylight is sucked out of this fun house, barely clinging to their disfigured faces.

Mothers suck on the smoothest sea glass that their children sift from the rocky beaches. They seal the jagged, opaque pieces in jam jars with fresh water for the mantle of Sunday's brunch, preserving the myths of a nature now on the run. Their smallest children beg to bring home the living snails that emerge from their sheaths to the harmonic hums of their tight little vocal cords.

Fireworks every Thursday, still going on after all these years. Old men steal snacks from their baby's babies. They dip tobacco into their cheeks, feeling a stinging tingle in each tooth's abscess. Sparks from beach fires fill the big dipper's spoon.

The sad clowns, with weak chins, stay after work to play with the baby chickens, the only leftover prize at the Ring Around the Coke Bottle stand. The happy clowns flirt with the cotton candy ladies, asking where they go for confession.

PROSPECTORS

M sits, mostly alone, on the cliff beach beside his father's house. He has not left this spot all afternoon and is unsure if his legs will move should he want them to. He's watching a crab the size of a soldier's hand trying to eat through a rotten piece of rope in which the poor soul is tangled. The tide is coming in, sloughing between M's toes and through the gnawing claws of the crab. Above him, on the lip of the fragile ledge, the Captain and the Tycoon seem to be excavating one of the deeper crevices.

M: Well, there you are. I thought I wouldn't see you again. I thought you'd be dead by now.

Captain: I was already dead, you ass.

Tycoon: Indeed, I died back in May, before the paint was dry on the ticket booth.

M: Leave us alone. [Three sets of sailor's feet emerge from beneath the pile of rope, which the crab is tangled in. M rests a hand on the shoulder of one sailor, while the others reach for his waist and the back of his neck] What good can you lot possibly bring here?

Tycoon: We're looking for you, sport. Wanna help you get back to normal.

M: If I needed your help, I would've come looking for you.

Captain: Should take the lifeline where you can or you might really lose it, starving and alone. [Pushes his right nostril closed and blows a thick wad of snot out of the left nostril. M can see a faint trace of blood in the mucus where it lands, between his bent and open knees]

When the Captain speaks, the wind blows. When the Tycoon opens his mouth, a big, brass band plays.

Tycoon: [Slapping the Captain on the shoulder] Quit fucking with the boy and keep digging. We're all getting hungry. [Without looking up] I see your new crew is quite friendly there, anybody gettin' lucky?

M: Whatever we win from each other disappears the next morning. I've been losing my memory each dawn.

Captain: Damn shame you didn't stay away when you had the fuckin' chance. What'd I tell you? Let yourself forget. Get gone and never come back.

Tycoon: Get gone and never come back.

M: Don't worry about me. Can one of you tell me my name?

Captain: [Grabs hold of something stuck deep in the crevice and begins to pull with all his weight] Got something. What do we have here?

Tycoon: [Smiles just beyond M, with his hand still on the Captain's shoulder. The band plays a national anthem, but not the one you might expect] Well, now. Here's the start of something. Get it out now, quick, before it loses its value and the kid forgets how much this is gonna sting.

With a final pull, the rock releases a dress the color of a burnt scab. M recognizes his mother's shape. One of the sailor's whispers something into M's neck. M can smell vodka and hard-boiled eggs in the air between them.

M: That's what you've been looking for? You tell me to forget everything and then you go and dig it all up.

Tycoon: I'm an excavator, son. It's my job to destroy while I pretend to improve.

Captain: Like that broke down fun park, you son of a bitch? I've got warts worth more than that piece of shit.

Tycoon: You better bite your rotten tongue; I don't need that shit from you. On its better days that park was the only thing that brought people here.

The Captain wraps the dress around his rump, shakes and shimmies to the anthem that grows louder every time the Tycoon opens his mouth. This is all one-part truth and one-part lie, dealt with the same blow.

M: [Listening once more to the whispers in his ear] Just a sad clown wasteland now, you old goat. Nothing there for my friends and I. [Nodding with our words] Lonely women who can't dance and [nodding harder with his eyes shut tight] too much debt. Nothing but an empty ghost ship. And I can't stand any more ghosts.

Tycoon: I should come down there and smack you senseless, boy. [Gestures as if getting up but slips on the wet rock and loses one leg into the crevice]

Captain: Idiot! Shut up and keep digging. [Still dancing along the edge with the dress, stepping on the hem with his muddy boots]

M: Tell me what you're looking for?

Tycoon: Almost got it now. Yes, sir.

Captain: The way! [The wind blows] The way to the bottom of the sea is paved in oil slicks lit by the flame of fictions. A son and his mother. Letters from...Letters from lover to lover. A language written far from here in bodies and dirt and fur. A whole genre of memory signed truly yours. So, your man left you? So, you pretend he is dead too and play grab ass with ghosts? Is that what you do to honor your dead?

M: [Eyes shut tight, squeezing a sailor's hand that isn't really there. We tap out rhythms on our exposed skin, trying to calm his nerves] I mourn for no one in the morning but by night I am blinded by the chorus.

Tycoon: [Yelling over the music, the band just plays louder] Almost got it now!

Captain: Well, I hope you are hungry tonight.

M: Tell me what you're looking for?

Tycoon: I'm hungry.

Captain: Hungry!

M: Please. What're you loo—

Captain: [Yelling over the wind] Starving now.

M: —king for?

The Tycoon reaches deep into the crevice, seeming to lift something of great weight. The sailors watch intently on M's behalf. What emerges first, a paw the size of a fisherman's hand, with dirty claws dripping in engine oil. Then a leg covered in matted fur and then a body with the head of a dog, grinning, with blood between its teeth and gums. A sailor whispers to M and he opens his eyes.

M: Hungry for—

Tycoon: [Laughing] Woo hoo, now let's eat the son of a bitch.

Captain: We'll sleep good tonight, bellies full of the bastard's memory.

M: [Sticks his toes in the claws of the crab, still stuck in the rope. He winces with each hard and desperate pinch] —for my father's history. And my mother's body. And this island's remedy. And my soldier's sweet, white teeth. And—

Captain: [Laughing. Launches the bloodied and muddied body at M and his sailors] Dead dog meat!

Dear M,

Nearing the end of our correspondence. I can't say for certain if we've ac-complished anything here. You still hear voices that I cannot access. I have given you a voice that now feels circumspect on even the brightest of days. You've adopted a talent for witness, a capacity to change shape, an ability to exist without having a voice. To feel the strain of a life lived in a basement of dreams. You let spiders bite you in your sleep because it makes your skin real upon waking.

So, you've found companionship, some real and others impossibly thin in the changing light. They will follow you and drive arrows through your eyelids. Go on then drift out to the desert once more where you think you'll find oasis. That is, memory crystallized. Some grime sticks so hard under your fingernails that you have to dig it out with your bottom teeth. So, you think somewhere else you'll become a better man. Take the bodies of the ones who've abandoned you and wrap yourself in them, then drown your-self with the milk of cactus roots. I grant you this and wish you many more secrets tapped out in the ripple of tides yet to come.

Remember that sly witch I once told you about? She has not stopped laugh-ing since last we were here. She has grown old and I fear her mind is completely lost. Her reflection in the ice looks like my own, looks like yours. She laughs drunkenly at my attempts to understand, to grasp you in these pages and define what keeps you alive in the dead of winter, on an island that is drifting out to sea. Cut the tree down, you'll say. Bear witness to her stomach stabbed with the tawny needles of every broken branch, her legs crushed by the thick thigh of this old tree. Splinter her story, and yours, and ours then glue it back together. A mosaic. Pieces of flesh sewn together with grapevines.

I can't say for certain. This is all I know, I really fear the laughing woman is me, grown old. Dying and unable to let go of her perch. Somehow a future becomes the past and a labor begins.

Yours truly,

C'EST MOI

M lights candles compulsively. Sometimes in his sleep. He cannot be alone without a touch of light. He cannot be alone without the scent of herbs and dried flowers sparking in wax.

Blue is his favorite kind of colored glass but he only collects the big hunks of yellow and brown, letting them collect dust on his windowsill. He doesn't admit he likes the unfinished pieces, with sharp edges. He's beginning to lose his sight.

M received a wire informing him that his mistress in the desert has finally died, in her sleep, her head on his pillow which she never washed after all these years.

Mourning by his side as ever, we encourage him to buy an antique teacup painted with blue flowers that he said reminded him of the woman who told him it was all going to be okay and who brought him the soldier. The cup was awkward, clunky really, and the handle so small he could fit only one slender finger through. *Just like her*. It seemed the perfect tribute.

We tried to tie the silk ribbon from the gift-wrapping around his wrist but we were all shaking too hard and gave up.

Nothing was said for two whole days.

AN OLD TIME GOOD BYE

We did not have much time left together. M could see that we were starting to fade. Our final supper: freshly caught crabs stolen from his neighbor's trap, figs and soft cheese, Campari and soda. He was going to leave directly after to avoid that missing memory of a night well spent and worse, that lingering outline of a feeling the next morning. He tried to convince himself he was ready for another goodbye, his peace so clearly implausible. But he had too many questions:

```
       .-- / .... / .- / - -..-. .- / .-. / . -..-. -.--
/ --- / ..- -..-. -.. / --- / .. / -. / --. -..-. ....
/ . / .-. / .
```

Playing with your fur, enjoying the mess and this pretend peace. We love the texture of your paper skin with glossy splashes of sweat. M, we will burn your memory on all the boulevards from California to Germany, melt your New England prudity with the heat. Let's all become caretakers of self-made selves.

```
       -.. / --- -..-. -.-. / --- / .-.. / --- / .-. /
... -..-. .-.. / --- / --- / -.- -..-. -.. / .. / ..-. /
..-. / . / .-. / . / -. / - -..-. - / --- -..-. -.-- /
--- / ..-
```

We can't say for certain how these colors appear to you, but we do know: a hipbone like yours is darker when seen from below and from now on we'll always dream in coarse blue of barnacles and hints of aging white hair and burnt skin.

```
       .-- / .. / .-.. / .-.. -..-. .. -..-. -- / .. /
... / ... -..-. -.-- / --- / ..-
```

You will always admire the way we rustled the dead leaves on our walks and our faded tattoos that you traced so gently again and again. We adore you, if you want us to return, you can always try whispering questions like these. Into the wind, let them fall in the surf or the dry horizon, wherever you may be. Perhaps we'll choose to find you again.

.. -..-. .-- / .. / .-.. / .-.. -..-. .-. / . /
-- / . / -- / -... / . / .-. -..-. -.-- / --- / ..-

But also, never forget the hundred games we learned how to play.

WANDERING ABANDON, WHICH IS SO AMERICAN

Someday, new iterations of men and women will invent better machines and a red button that preserves what we smell. What we taste. Someday, these machines will remind M of how he touched a soldier's body tucked deep within some version of Babylon, at dusk, on a Sunday. What that felt like.

M will always hate the smell of fish, but he enjoys the greasy feel of hot butter and lemon juice. He will kill anything for his many loves, do anything a soldier demands, which is a lie he tells himself and we overhear. He would gut any fish, wait for its final scream and then ignore it if it meant he could live forever.

We cannot erase M's dreams, painted on a canvas the texture of driftwood.

We share his fingerprint and his mother's skirts will stay wrapped around our waist on cold nights to come. These objects that M once lived with. These things don't exist just anywhere. If constellations look different in Dogtown it's so he can better recall the landscape later, when no one is left to ask him where he is going or if he needs anything at all.

M rides out with the tide for good, out of Dogtown. His home. The place of sailors, sunken boats, graves and graves.

He leaves the island only after we, the Sailors, disappear from his bed. We return to our vessel, and leave the harbor drawn on a map behind his eyes.

He burns his palms with a bundle of dried sage, left to him in a wealthy woman's will.

We leave him to search for his self once again.

Oil kills oil. Skin hairs rub each other to sleep as winter approaches.

M finishes a cigarette, flicks it out the window of the car he is driving.

The desert is cracking apart. Sirens sound out lost words behind his ears. Thinking he will never smell the ocean again. Cactus is the sea-weed of the west. The honeybees drown in it. He is looking for the soldier, for her, for himself as always and calls out using all the wrong names because now there are too many.

Distracted by a shadow, he stains the road with the body of a small rabbit.

ACKNOWLEDGEMENTS

Thank you Jeffrey DeShell for the mentorship I needed to believe in and finish this book, for your honesty and conviction. To Ruth Ellen Kocher, for your poetic force and guidance. Elisabeth Sheffield, Marcia Douglas, and Victor LaValle who put eyes on this in its early days and said *yes, keep going*. My chosen family of readers from New York to Maine, Colorado cohort, caregivers to my children, and residency kin at Martha's Vineyard Institute of Creative Writing and Tin House; your love, time, and patience were everything; thank you.

To *The Ekphrastic Review* for publishing 'Still Life' and championing the vital romance between the visual and literary arts. Thank you, Jesi Buell and the team at Kernpunkt Press, for working so tirelessly to publish experimental work that might otherwise be lost.

Thank you, Marsden, for showing me a way in. Edie and Arlo, in the midst of all this you changed me and it is because of you that I was able to claim this language as my own. To Ben, my gratitude always and my greatest love of all.

LOIE RAWDING was born in 1987 and raised on the coast of Maine. Individual writings and mixed media work have been featured in *SAND* (Berlin), *The Ekphrastic Review* (Toronto), *Map Literary*, *Anamesa*, *DREGINALD*, and *Lemon Hound* (Montreal), among others. She is a Pushcart Prize nominee and has held residencies at the Martha's Vineyard Creative Writing Institute and Tin House. Loie is a Teaching Artist with The Porch Writers Collective. She divides her time between Cliff Island, Maine and Nashville, Tennessee.

For more: www.loierawding.com

www.ingramcontent.com/pod-product-compliance
Lightning Source LLC
Chambersburg PA
CBHW072356020726
47506CB00004B/1144